Fl

"Zorg
"Yeah, Drew?"
"What are we doing in England?"
"Going to have a little fun."

The ship started moving again, flying over the fields. It buzzed a farmhouse, then took off for the sky again.

The ship kept flitting around, and every once in a while it would get close to a house or something. But once, when the ship got really close to this, like, white-colored cottage, the lights came on and this old guy came out of the front door carrying a gun. It looked like a shotgun. He pointed it at the ship.

BLAM!

Wow, the guy let loose with both barrels.

Zorg and Flez fell on the floor laughing. Then I started to laugh. There was this scrawny guy in baggy underwear, shooting at us. I mean, was this guy lame or what. Did he think he was going to bag a Flying Saucer? The guy was a moron. I guess he never thought he might be starting a space war by doing that, taking potshots at aliens. What a jerk.

Some people have no consideration.

Living with Aliens

by John DeChancie

Ace Books by John DeChancie

The Castle Series

CASTLE PERILOUS
CASTLE FOR RENT
CASTLE KIDNAPPED
CASTLE WAR!
CASTLE MURDERS
CASTLE DREAMS
CASTLE SPELLBOUND
BRIDE OF THE CASTLE

The Skyway Trilogy

STARRIGGER
RED LIMIT FREEWAY
PARADOX ALLEY

THE KRUTON INTERFACE
LIVING WITH ALIENS

Living with Aliens

John DeChancie

ACE BOOKS, NEW YORK

This book is an Ace original edition,
and has never been previously published.

LIVING WITH ALIENS

An Ace Book / published by arrangement with
the author

PRINTING HISTORY
Ace edition / April 1995

All rights reserved.
Copyright © 1995 by John DeChancie.
Cover art by Danilo Ducak.
This book may not be reproduced in whole or in part,
by mimeograph or any other means, without permission.
For information address: The Berkley Publishing Group,
200 Madison Avenue, New York, NY 10016.

ISBN: 0-441-00204-8

ACE®
Ace Books are published by The Berkley Publishing Group,
200 Madison Avenue, New York, NY 10016.
ACE and the "A" design are trademarks
belonging to Charter Communications, Inc.

PRINTED IN THE UNITED STATES OF AMERICA

10 9 8 7 6 5 4 3 2 1

This one is for Ron Hankison,
Dr. Vague,
and Clonedog

CHAPTER # 1

I dont know where to start so I guess starting at the beginning is OK. My name is Drew Hayes and I live at 3489 Manor Drive in Keynesville, Ohio 41379. I am 13 years old. I have a sister. She is 16 and a brother, he is 7. The reason I am writing this is a couple of them but mostly just to keep a record of everything thats happened and maybe just for myself, so I remember stuff in case I ever want to write a book, because they said they would pay me a lot of money to write one. I called some publishers in New York and a lady told me that if I had an important story, maybe they would publish it if I wrote a book. But I said no. The reason I said no was because the lady said maybe if the story was big enough and they wanted to publish it as a book, they'd hire some guy to write it for me. And I said no way. If anyone is going to write it, then I am. I have a "word processor". It makes writing real easy and quick though I havent learned to do everything with it yet like spellchecking but I am a pretty good speller anyway. I get OK grades in school, which is Keynesville Middle School. Next year I start Highschool. I'm looking forward to taking Highschool subject's like higher math and driving. I want to drive and one day I'd like to own my own car, possibly a BMW or a Lexus.

But that is beside the point. I better start at the beginning again. What happened was that aliens came to live with us. Two of them, and there names were Zorg and Flez. I'd better start at the beginning. I've said that several times now. Its kind of hard to tell where the "beginning" really is, because of several factors, the main one is because the aliens make you forget stuff sometimes. Like they have some ability to play with your mind and you do'nt even know their there. Thats what was really hard about all this, most people didnt even see them most of the time. Until everyone started seeing them, but that was later. At first no one saw them not even us. I mean our family, my Dad, even though he isn't, he's my stepfather, and my Mom, and my brother and sister. Well, Dad isn't really our stepfather either, because he and Mom aren't married yet. They will be, though, they say. Sometime next year. But they have been saying that for a long time. But nevermind, that's not important now.

But maybe it is important. So I'd better go into it. Dad's name is Nathan Ziegler and he used to do a lot of things, like sell cars, and then insurance, and then real estate, and then Amway, and then used cars again, but now he writes poetry and is getting himself together and finding spiritual things, and like that. That's how we met the aliens, driving up to the Men's Inner Vision Retreat Camp that he was at, to pick him up, because he and his buddies got in an argument with the guy who drove the bus, over money or something, so they missed the bus back, but it was okay Mom said, because it was a nice drive up there anyway, in Pennsylvania in the mountains, where the Camp was.

I have a real Dad, or father. He's dead, though. He died in 1984 when his truck went off the Interstate and hit a diner, but miraculessly nobody in the diner was killed, but he was. They don't know why he went off the road and hit the diner but it might have been he was asleep. He drove a lot and got tired. I don't remember him much but I miss him anyway.

Anyway. Nathan is a nice guy, he treats us real good. He never yells or anything, except at the TV when the talk shows are on. He is real involved in issues and politics. But even more than that, he likes spiritual things. Which is why he was at the Men's Retreat. He says there is not enough spiritualism in the United States. We are to materialistic, and were killing the environment. And the O-zone. There's a big hole in the O-zone and its going to kill us, Nathan says. Man have been raping the planet for to long and killing whales. Nathan likes whales, there are a lot of pictures of whales at our house. He belongs to all those groups that protect whales. Funny though, he's never seen one, though he says he's going out to California some day and go on the whale watch boats. He likes all animals, which is why he is a vegetarian, though he eats eggs, even though their bad for his colesterall, he says. But he eats them which is why he's not a real Vegan vegetarian, but he's working on that. He says he wants to be like the Janes. They are a sext in India that doesnt eat any animals, or even step on any insects. The Janes wear vales in front of there faces so they dont breath in any fleas or natts. I think that is pretty silly but he says their very spiritual, only maybe a little extreme.

Like I said, Nathan's an OK guy and he doesnt give me or my sister Delores any trouble. Delores's nickname is Lori, we call her Lori. My little brother is named Tyler, after our Great-Grandfather Tyler Eustace Biggs, who was a judge in Dayton. He was a hanging judge, Nathan says. I think he's joking. My mother's name is Cheryl Biggs Hayes. She says she wont change it again if she marries Nathan. Thats okay, because I don't particularly like Ziegler as a name. I mean it's OK, but I'd rather keep Hayes, which I would anyway. Kids dont have to change thier names when their mothers re-marry.

Anyway, that's my family, Cheryl, Nathan, me, Lori, and Tyler. And that's who met the aliens that night when we were coming back from Pennsylvania. Where it was exactly that we met them, I don't really know, but it was somewhere on Interstate Route 80, but off on a side road. It was late and we were looking for an open gas station, because the gas gauge on my Mom's Toyota is broke, and Nathan taught her to zero the trip odometer and get the tank filled when it gets to 300 miles, since the car gets an average of 30 miles to the gallon and has a 10 gallon gas tank. The gas guage was reading something like 640 miles and she forgot to zero it the last time she got filled up, and she did'nt remember what the reading was when she put gas in before we left to pick up Nathan, but she knows she only put five dollars worth of gas in, because her credit card was overlimit and she didnt have much cash. So Nathan said you'd better get some gas. But the station was closed, and Mom was worried we were going to run out of gas out here in the middle of nowhere. But Nathan wasn't worried because he knew there was all kinds of truck stops and anyway the Ohio Turnpike was'nt very far away, so he told Mom to keep driving, which we had to do anyway, seeing as there was nothing else we could do. Nathan said mom ha'dnt drove that far and there was probably lots of gas in the tank, not to worry.

So were driving back down the road to get back on the Interstate, when all of a sudden there was this light in the sky, real bright. It wasn't a star or anything, because it moved, and it wasnt a plane because the lights didn't flash and it did'nt make any noise. It came up over the trees and it hoovered over us, following us and shining this really bright light down on the car. It was like blinding. Mom screamed and said what is that, Nathan? Nathan had his head out the window on his side, trying to look up at the thing. It's big Nathan yelled! Is it a helocopter my Mom said? No its not Nathan yelled back! So what is it my Mom screamed? She was scared and so was I and so was Lori. She screamed too. I didnt scream but I wanted to. It was like, I don't know why I was scared because nothing was happening except that light shining on us and we couldn't see anything and there was no sound or anything, but I was scared anyway.

Nathan said you better pull over but my Mom said she was too scared, but she started slowing down and veering off the road anyway and pretty soon we were on the shoulder, and it wasn't a good shoulder. It had bumps. So it was getting bumpy. Meanwhile the thing, whatever it was, was still over us and shining the light, and Nathan was still trying to look up but the light was too bright and he said the F word. He doesn't say the F word much but he says it and sometimes around Tyler. Tyler says it now, sometimes. Anway, he says the F word, like what is that F-ing thing? He didn't know. None of us knew what it was. We were pretty scared, but I guess I said that already.

Mom still didn't stop the car, and I was worried we were going to run into a tree, but she finally stopped. Go the other way Nathan yelled! So, she turned the steering wheel and the car rolled all the way around and we went the the other way, and this was the funny thing, the thing didn't follow us. We raced back down where we came from, and the thing, it sort of went off to the left behind some trees, like real fast, and dissappeared. Boy was I releived! Wow that was wierd Nathan said. Yeah, really.

We passed the closed gas station again and Nathan told Mom to turn around, so she did. She was really nervous and said, Nathan you drive. Okay, Nathan said, and she stopped and he got out and came around, and got behind the wheel. We started off again toward the Interstate. There was no sign of the bright thing.

God, what was that thing Mom said? A UFO, of course, Nathan said. Dont you know a UFO when you see one? I asked Nathan how to spell it and he told me, but it's really easy because its just the letters. It stands for "Unidentifeid Flying Object."

Lori was crying. She was really afraid, but I didn't know what to say except that the thing was gone, so I said that, but she was still scared. I wasn't worried because Nathan was driving now and he's a pretty good driver. Men are usually better drivers and not as afraid, but you can't say that because it's sexist. So women are pretty good drivers too and their not so afraid either. Mom was doing pretty good. Tyler didnt seem afraid much. He said the F word, repeating what Nathan said What is that F-ing thing?

Mom didn't even here it. She was still looking off to the side of the road in the trees. It was real dark.

Suddenly, it came back over the trees but from a different direction. Nathan swerved and went off the road and screeched the tires. We stopped inside a little area off the road, a pull off, and there were some trees hiding us.

It was sending this bright search beam into the trees. Nathan turned off the engine and doused the headlights. We still couldn't see what the heck it was, and now there were trees in the way. All it was, was pretty big, and it shined like a searchlight in addition to sending out like these bright rays. The woods lit up like they were on fire or it was day or something. I was scared all over again. But not as much because it seemed to have lost us now. We were right there down the road a little ways, and it must be able to see us, but it didnt spot us. I was real worried that it would, though.

It searched and searched, and it kept moving in the sky, floating back and forth. Jeez, that thing is big Nathan said. Bigger than I thought. Those bright rays kept on coming out.

It did that for like five minutes. And then it started to float off to the left.

Then it really hightailed out of there, like it was the fastest thing I ever saw. Shoosh!! It shot off like a rocket, only no stuff came out the back, like the Space Shuttle. It wasnt' like that. And again it didnt make any noise. Wow. We all watched it. It became like a bright star, then a faint star. And then it was gone.

We all breathed a sigh of releif. Lets get going Mom said! Before it comes back!

Nathan gunned the Toyota and we peeled out of there and headed back towards the highway.

But there was somebody standing by the side of the road, two guys. They looked funny. Well, they really didn't look all that funny, they were just short. Like about 4 feet and some inch's tall. That's not so short, but they were grownup guys, you could tell, because they were bald, mostly, except the sides of their head. Thier hair there was pretty long but not real long. They were dressed in these loud shirts, Hawiian shirts, and dark trousers and wing tip shoes. I couldn't see all this right away, but Nathan slowed and we could see them in the headlights standing right on the edge of the road, with one foot out and their thumbs up. They were hitchhiking. Behind them was this humongous suitcase or duffel bag or something, but it looked kind of funny.

Where did these guys come from Nathan asked? My Mom said she was glad somebody else saw that because nobody else would believe it.

I'll be damned Nathan said. Where were these jokers when the thing was up there? Nobody knew. They must have been there all the time, or hiding in the trees.

I have to tell you now, since you already probably guessed, that these were the aliens, but we didn't know it then. We were dumb.

We passed them, and then Nathan pulled over to the shoulder and stopped. The guys walked up to the car. I looked out the window. The little guys were carring the big duffel bag between them, but it didn't look heavy, just bulky. They came up to Nathan's window and said hello. Both of them said that.

Now we could see them real good and Tyler laughed. I laughed too because they both looked like Danny DeVito. Really. It was uncanny! They were the spittin image of Danny DeVito, both of them. That was really strange. And it was even stranger when they talked, because they sounded exactly like Danny DeVito, like the TV was on and you were watching "Taxi" or the VCR with one of his movies.

The one closer to Nathan said Hi, were lost! And Nathan said Where do you want to go? And the guy said Where do you people live, and Nathan said Ohio. The first guy looked at the other guy and then said We want to go to Ohio. Well, Nathan said Do you want a lift? And the guy nodded his head and the other guy nodded his head too. Yeah, that would be really nice the first guy said. Okay Nathan said and got out of the car, because he had seen the big bag but now he was wondering what we were going to do because the bag was too big to fit into the trunk of the Toyota. Nathan helped them lug it and he said what the heck do you guys have in hear, a tank? The guys laughed. They laughed a lot. Like giggling. It was a funny kind of giggle. It didn't sound right. What I mean by that sometimes it soudned like a bird. But not really. Do you know what I mean? No you dont. Anyway, they were always giggling.

So Nathan figured out how we could lug the thing by strapping it to the roof, because in the trunk there were bungee cords and ropes. I helped to tie off the thing on the side to the rear door handles. It looked funny sitting up there, but it was fassened securely and it wasnt going anywhere, as long as Nathan didnt go 100 miles per hour or anything.

Tyler got in the front seat between Mom and Nathan, and the aliens squeezed in with me and Lori in the back. They smelled funny, but I couldn't really say what they smelled like. They didnt smell bad. Just funny. They both smiled at us. I smiled back and then looked at Lori and she was looking at them, like, who are these guys? She looked at me funny, but I'm like, what am I supposed to say?, besides I couldnt say anything with them right there. I didnt think anything about Nathan picking them up because Nathan is always saying we should give that guy a ride when he sees a hitchiker. Mom never wants to because shes afraid. Woops, there I go again with sexism. But she is. She doesnt trust nobody where Nathan always wants to be kind and feel sorry for somebody. That is the way Nathan is. But this time what I should have thought about was why Mom didnt say, no, dont pick them up, especially these two weirdoes. I mean, they didnt look like aliens then but they sure did look strange. I mean who would of thought that two guys could both look like Danny DeVito?

Nathan was thinking the same thing because he asked Are you guys twins? And the first guy who spoke said no, why, do we look alike. Then they giggled and we all laughed. Actually they seemed pretty nice guys. But we didn't ask them about how they looked or anything after that. As time went on they didnt look so much like Danny DeVito, until finally they— But that comes later.

Where are you from asked Mom? The first guy said they were from another country. And I asked what country. And he talked to the other guy for a second, but I couldn't get what he said. And then he said Mexico. Oh, Mom said. Mexico's a long way away. Yeah, the guy said. They were hitch hiking, and they came up all the way from Mexico. They were looking for work.

When they said Mexico it made sense how they looked a little, because we went to Mexico in 1990 and some Mexicans are shorter than Americans. Especially the Indians of Mexico. Not all of them but some of them. So it made sense. But it didnt make sense that they spoke such good English. They sounded American. So I asked them why if there were from Mexico why they spoke such good English, and the second guy said We've been up here a lot. And I said Oh.

So we drove all the way back to Ohio with them. They didn't say much, and neither did we. But that's the way it is on long trips, everybody just sits and looks out the window, even when it's night, and of course Tyler fell asleep as soon as we got back on the Interstate, and then Lori fell asleep, and then I think I did, but I'm not sure. Because the next thing I knew we were driving down our street, Manor Drive, and Nathan pulled the car into the driveway and he hit the garage door opener, which was on the sunvisor, and the garage door opened, and he drove right in without stopping, and we were home. I looked and the two guys were still with us. I dont know why Nathan drove right home with them but I guess he was talking to them while we were sleeping, so I guess I was asleep after all.

Mom woke up and picked up Tyler and got out, and I helped her out. I woke up Lori. She sleeps like a log, and she's hard to wake up sometimes, especially for school. And times like this. I shook her hard and she swore at me, nothing bad, just leave me alone you little butthead. Mom told her to wake up. Then she wakes up and looks at the little guys, and she says, are we home? And I say yes, and she looks at them and rubs her eyes. What are they doing here she asks?

Then Nathan said these guys dont have a place to stay so I offered to put them up for the night. I hope you dont mind, Cheryl.

Mom was still holding Tyler, but she says, why, no, not if they dont have a place to stay. They can sleep in the game room, and she asks them, is that alright?

The little guys nodded their heads and said, sure, that's great! We won't be any trouble.

Im sure you wont, Mom said. Then she brought Tyler upstairs and she didnt come back down.

So we took the big duffel bag off the Toyota and helped the little guys tote it into the gameroom. It almost didnt fit through the door. It was colored silver and it didnt have zippers or anything, but it had handles. I couldn't see an opening or how you would get into it. But it was none of my business.

I guess you guys can both fit on this couch Nathan said. If you lay at both ends with your feet in. They tried it and they fit. You guys have sleeping bags? No? So Nathan went upstairs and got them some sheets. It was a warm night. It was July, if I didn't mention it. So they didn't need blankets or anything.

So Nathan just stood there looking at them for a minute,

and I did too. Boy, they were pretty strange guys. And they looked like you know who. (I won't say it again, because it's tiresome. Besides, like I said, as time went on, they looked different.)

So, you need anything, just ask said Nathan.

They said Thanks, we really appreciate this.

Nathan said, sure. So Nathan and I went upstairs.

CHAPTER TWO

I've been writing this wrong. I should use quotes when people are talking "like this". But I'm not going back and changing all that in the first chapter. I'm dividing this into chapters, just like a book. I want it to be as much like a book as I can make it, so maybe those New York publishers will buy it.

Mom had to go to work the next morning. Mom is a secretary and works for the Central Ohio Consorteum for Art, which is a charitable and nonprofit place. They have an Art Gallery and a Crafts Center. Mom doesn't make much money, but it's enough to pay the mortagage, which Dad left, my other dad. The real one. But he was heavily insured, so we don't need much. He left us "well provided". Nathan contributes to the house too, but he's always complaining about money. He never has much. It's the economy. The economy is pretty bad in Ohio. There used to be two factories around Keynesville, but both closed. "It's those corporate jerks". Thats what Nathan says. Sending "our jobs across the border to Mexico".

But now we had two Mexicans right in the house, and Nathan didnt seem particularly ticked off at them. In fact he was real kind to them, offering to put them up. We even fed them in the morning. Though they didnt eat much. I thought that was strange. They sniffed and smelled everything. Mom made blueberry pancakes and non-meat bacon (made from soybeans) and hash browns, and they nibbled here and there. I watched them. They asked what this was and that was. I told them. I said "don't they have food like that in Mexico"? and they shook thier heads.

Right then I didn't understand something. They were Mexican and you-know-who is Eytalian. So why did they look Eytalian if they were Mexican? Of course, I don't exactly know what Eyetalians looks like, except for Brandon Marscapone down the street, he's Eytalian, but he didn't look like you-know-who. I was in Mexico so I knew what Mexicans looked like. Funny, they don't look like those guys in the movies wearing sombreros and blankets and with ammo belts criscrossed over their chests, and have bad teeth. Anyway, these little guys didnt look like real Mexicans or movie ones.

But it didnt bother me particularly, any of that. So I ate my fake bacon and hash browns and one pancake. I don't like pancakes so much.

Then I realized something. I didn't know these guys names. Last night there wasn't time and I fell asleep and did'nt talk to them much, but we didnt know their names. I wondered about that. I wondered if Nathan knew thier names, but he didn't say anything.

Anyway, we finished eating.

Nathan asked if the guys "needed a lift anywhere, like out to the highway to hitch hike," but they said "no, they could walk".

Nathan asked them "how are you going to tote that big sachel of yours"? and they said they would "manage it". Nathan just shook his head.

The little guys went back down stairs after thanking Mom for the breakfast. They were always polite little guys to

Mom. "They probably have everything they own in that bag" Mom said. Nathan said "yeah probably".

It was summer so I didn't have school. Usually I would go down the street to Damon Zabinski's house and go in the back and shoot hoops. Or maybe we would go swimming at the county pool, or go over to Brandon Marscapone's house. Brandon has a pool, an above ground one.

But I didn't feel like doing anything. So I went up to my room and played with my video games for awhile. Then I came back down stairs.

"Where are they"? I said to Nathan, because Mom wasnt there. "Your mother drove them to the bus stop" Nathan said. "I worry about those guys" he said. "Why"? I said. "I don't know, they looked lost and a little afraid to me, like babes in the woods". Then Nathan sighed and said "but I guess their's nothing we can do. Theyl'l probly be caught and deported." I said what's that mean? And he said they'll send them back to Mexico. Why I said? Nathan said "their illegal", and I said How come?" and Nathan said "There illegal aliens. They cant enter this country without a Visa. And I said thats really dumb. Just because they dont have a Visa? What if they have MasterCard? And Nathan threw back his head and laughed. No you dont understand, a permit is what they need, a permit to live here. I said "Oh".

"Well, that's that" Nathan said and went back to reading his book. He's allways reading a book. I don't read much. I usually watch TV. I know I should read more books, and sometimes I do, if it's about sports or something interesting. But most of it is boring. Books, I mean, especially what they want you to read in school. My sister reads books, though. She reads those Romance books that always has the woman on the cover with her dress half off and the guy has muscles like Arnold Shwartzinager and their kissing and hugging. I read one of them and it was silly. There was sex but it didnt say anything dirty. Brandon's dad gets the magazines with the women with big breasts in it and he brings them over sometimes or I go over to his place and we read them.

Really we look at the pictures. Thats where I learned that grownup women have hair between their legs just like guys, but of course they dont have the other stuff. Some of these pictures have guys in them but they dont like really show anything. And some of them have GIRLS naked together. Wow! Thats sexy. I get a real bone when I look at that stuff.

I better not write anymore about that in case Mom reads this. It could be embarassing.

Anyway I forget what I did for the rest of the day. I probably shot hoop's over at Damons or read comic books or sat and watched his big screen TV. Wow is it big. It covers the whole wall and has stereo. We dont have anything like that. Or maybe we listened to CD's. I forget.

Anyway I came home and Nathan cooked dinner. I forget what that was too. Nathan is a vegetarian and he always cooks vegetables. I hate vegetables, but some of them are good. He makes potatoes that are pretty good. But the green stuff is usally yucky, like Brocoli. Wow that stuff stinks and sometimes he eats it raw. Yuck! The beans are okay. He cooks things like beans and rice with tomatos, and that's not too bad. But other times he makes curry and I HATE that. Or saffron rice. It looks like somebody peed in it. But Nathan says it's all good for you and has lots of vitamins and newtrients. Well OK, Nathan. But I'd rather eat hot dogs and fries and pork chops and mash potatos with lots of gravey, and hamburgers. Nathan says all thats poison. Plastic junk. It's toxic, it has dioxygen in it and colesterall. Pork is the worst thing you can eat because it has pig fat. Why its the worst thing I dont know he never says. But everytime mom cooks a pork chop I think about it. Mom still eats meat but Nathan never says anything. She doesn't eat meat much, just sometimes. And when she does she cooks it for us.

As I was saying, I really dont remember what I did that day or that night, but it was about midnight that the little guys came back.

I didnt wake up first, Nathan did. He went downstairs when the doorbell rang. I woke up and the doorbell was ringing but I was so sleepy I didnt get up right away. I looked over at Tyler's bed and he was still asleep. Then I got up and went to the stairs, and I heard the little guys talking. Nathan said, Sure go right downstairs, you know where everything is. Then the little guys went down stairs to the game room.

I waited until Nathan came up the stairs and I asked him, "Did they come back." He nodded and said "Yes". "Why did they I asked?" "They couldnt get a ride to Washington D.C." "Oh," I said. "Is that where they want to go"? "Yeah", Nathan said. "They want to go to Washington DC now. First they wanted to go to California, but now they want to go to DC." Nathan shook his head. "I can't figure them. Doesnt make sense." What doesn't I asked? "Well, they're names, for instance. Zorg and Flez. Those are'nt Spanish names. I don't think their really from Mexico". Where are they from do you think? "Possibly Eastern Europe" Nathan said. "Bosnia".

I didnt know where Bosnia was except I hear it on the news. So I just shrugged. "Maybe Checkaslovokia" Nathan said. "What I'll do, though, is contact a refugee agency I know. They may be able to help them."

So that was that and I went back to bed.

The next morning Zorg and Flez came up for breakfast. Mom didnt look very happy. She was wondering about these guys. I guess you cant blame her. But she cooked waffles and eggs and fake bacon. Nathan didnt eat the eggs. And the two little guys didnt eat again, just sniffed and tasted and like that. It was silly to watch.

I have to say something about how these guys talked. I said they sounded like the little Eytalian guy actor, and they did. But when they talked, it was funny. I mean it was really funny. I've been saying that they talked but they didnt really. What I mean is it sounded like a recording. I know thats crazy. I cant say how that sounds but I know it when I hear it. It wasn't like obvious or anything, you didnt even think about it when you heard them, but later you thought, boy that sounded funny. Like tinny? Or something, like it was a movie. Only

Boy, this is hard to discribe! I wish I was better with words.

Nathan didnt eat anything, but he drank coffee, and he sat there drinking it and looking at the two little guys.

We finished eating and it was like the day before, I went upstairs and this time I think I just sat around while Tyler watched cartoons on the TV in our room. It was Saturday and Mom did'nt work so she was downstairs.

I went back down stairs and then went down to the game room and Zorg and Flez were watching the TV in the game room. We have four TV's in the house. One in my and Tyler's room, one in Mom's and Nathan's room, one in the living room and one in the basement. One was Nathan's when he moved in. That's his in the game room, and it doesn't work too good but it's hooked up to cable. Anyway, the little guys were watching it. They were watching wrestling. They were laughing at it. I didnt see what was so funny. Then I thought they were'nt just laughing at it, they were enjoying it. Like they were delighted with it. They liked it alot. So I watched it with them for a little while. Then I went out to play.

When I came back the little guys were still watching TV, but it was the home shopping channel this time. Then one of them flipped the channel with the remote. Then I couldn't tell them apart but I think it was Zorg who had the remote. What came up next was the Christian channel, and they watched that. They didn't laugh at that and I dont think they liked it. Zorg flipped the remote again. Now it was a movie but I didn't know what it was, some old movie. Then they watched a auto racing, then golf, then Star Trek. They watched this for a while and it looked like they were interested in it.

I got tired of watching tv and went upstairs. Later I went to a movie with Damon and Brandon. I forget what the heck one it was, but it was one with Arnold Shcwarttenzennager.

He makes a lot of movies, and it wasnt one of them where he plays a robot and shoots up the place, it was different. It had lots of action, though. But I cant really remember it for some reason. Anyway, Nathan picked us up. Damon's father took us but Nathan picked us up in his van. It's one with three seats and when we got in Zorg and Flez were in the back seat, just sitting there, smiling at us. Damon looked at Brandon and then at me, but I didnt say anything. So we drove home.

Nathan let Brandon and Damon off up the street. When we pulled into our driveway I asked Nathan if he was going to drop off the guys anywhere. Nathan said that they really weren't ready to leave yet. If they got picked up on the highway by the police, then they might turn them over to Immigration. I asked what that was and Nathan told me, it's an agency that deals with aliens.

I asked him about the refugge place and he said it's in Columbus, he'd have to drive the guys there. "We dont get a whole heck of alot of aliens in Ohio" Nathan said. Except for a few coming down from Canada.

When Zorg and Flez went back down to the basement I asked Nathan why they were riding with him to pick us up at the movies. He said "They were just sitting down there all day watching TV and I thought they might want to go out for a spell".

I said "Oh".

The next day was Sunday and I went over to my Aunt's. It was my cousin Jordy's birthday, he's a year younger than me. It was OK. Nathan didn't come. Then Mom drove home and I watched TV in my room. Then I watched a movie on video tape, and then I went to bed.

The funny thing was this. Next day at dinner we were talking about weather we were going to New Jersey to the beach that summer, or to Lake Erie, for a vacation. I hate Lake Erie. But we were talking it over, and Mom said maybe we couldn't go to the beach this year, what with the economy, when all of a sudden she stops and looks at Nathan, and says, "Where are Zorg and Flez?"

And just then I remember that I had forgotten all about them being in the house. Like, it was as if they weren't there. But now I remembered. And Nathan said "Their up in the spare bedroom". And Mom said "What!" And Nathan said "Well it was kind of hard for them down there, no privacy" And Mom said "Privacy? What, are you telling me their're moving in?" And Nathan said "Temperarily." And Mom looked at him, and then she looked at me, and I shrugged. Then she looked at Nathan again. She looked like she was going to say something, but she didn't. I was wondering about it, myself. When were these guys going to get a life. Hey? I mean, really.

CHAPTER NO. "3"

I showed this to Mr. Olander, my English and Social Sceince teacher, and he says I'm doing it all wrong. The dialog, that is. Dialog should be a certain way in a story or book.

"You should put what people say on a separate line, like this" Mr. Olander said, and then he showed me on the word processer in school.

"Like this"?, I said.

"Yeah", Mr. Olander said "and you should put a comma between what people say and the word "said", said Mister Olander.

And then he showed me how to do it, but I have trouble keeping it straight, but I guess if I practice.

Mr. Olander is a Gay Man. When he told everybody, last year, the School Board was going to kick him out. He didn't tell everybody, actually. He said it to some reporter and it was in the newspaper. Only he claims he never said it to the reporter. But the reporter put it in the paper anyway. He says the reporter "OUT-ed him". The reporter says that's not true, that Mister Olander told him about it and he wrote it in the newspaper, but Mr. Olander keeps saying that the reporter "OUT"-ed him, and that the reporter is Gay too. Anyway, it's okay if Mr. Olander's Gay. It doesn't make any difference to me. But there was this big fight at the School Board and they're still talking about it, and some Christian people are saying he should be fired, and that was when there was this demonstration at the school by the Gay Rights Group, and the fist-fights, and a couple of people got beat up, but that was all on the 6 O'Clock News, and anyway it's boring. Mr. Olander is a nice guy. He's quiet and he's one of the teachers who doesn't yell much. Or any.

So anyway I showed him what I was writing and he gave me some tips on dialogue.

"Do you like to write, Drew", he asked?

"Yeah" I said, " Sure". "Sort of", I added.

"Did you ever think about being a writer when you get out of school"? he asked?

I said, "I never thought about it. How much money do they make?"

"Not very much, I'm afraid. Unless you write best-sellers, the pay is peanuts", Mr. Olander said.

"Then I don't want to be a writer" I said, "because I want to make lots of money and buy a Mercedes deisel".

He laughed. "Not a lot of writers drive Mercedes's" Mr. Olander said, "Deisel or otherwise. Nor do Teacher's, for that matter. I ought to know, I'm both. A Teacher and a Writer".

He told me that he's been trying to get published for years. He likes to write mysteries, plus other stuff. Poetry too. He wrote five mystery novels but none of them got published. Then he got discuoraged and quit.

"Its really hard to get started writing novels" he said, "or anything, even short stories. I've been sending stuff to the New Yorker and the Atlantic for years. Years"!.

Well, I dont really want to be a writer, but I figure I have to keep this up, because it's a good story, and people should know about it.

Mr. Olander couldn't show me how to run my Spellchecker. I keep trying to run it but I get an "error message". It says

"DICTIONARY NOT LOADED" but I don't know what that means, except that I know it's on the hard disk in the computer, because I put it there, so it's real hard to figure out.

"So, this thing about the UFO" Mr. Olander said, "is that a story or did that really happen?"

I told him it really happened.

"And the two wetbacks"?

"Huh"? I said.

"The Mexican twins. Is that true or is that something you made up"? Mr. Olander asked.

"That's true, too" I said.

"Really? Hmm". Mr. Olander just looked me.

Mr. Olander said if I wanted to be a writer I should read. So I went to the library and got out some books. I got out THE CALL OF THE WILD and some books on sports and SPACE CADET by Robert A. Heinlien. I liked the "CALL OF THE WILD" but I didnt finish it. I read a couple of chapters of 'SPACE CADET' by Robert A. Hienlen but I didn't finish it either. It wasn't so great, but it was well written. Then I read the sports books, and I finished one of them, but it was lousy.

Basically I dont like to read. I'd rather do other stuff. But I have to write this, so I guess I will continue reading books. The stuff they have in school is lousy, though. Boy, some of it really stinks, especially the girl's books. That's real dumb stuff. There always about horses. Who cares about horses anyway?

Anyway, Zorg and Flez started living with us, up in the spare bedroom, which was Nathan's writing room, or office. He moved out his desk and computer and an old two-seater couch and some boxes and books and put it all in the game room, and he gave them the bedroom. But there were no beds in there. We didn't have any to give them. Mom borrowed a footon from a lady down the street, and I gave

Zorg my sleeping bag and gave Tyler's to Flez. We don't ever go camping anyway, so we didn't need them.

Your probably wondering how we could tell them apart, but we could. Zorg and Flez looked different, only it wasn't a big difference. But there was a differnce. I can't say what the differnce was, but we could tell them apart alright. Once I learned which was which, it was easy.

By now your wondering too, what the heck was in the big duffel bag? Well, I found out. But it wasn't til a couple of days later.

Before that happened, the guys pretty much stayed up in the room. They didn't go out much, except when Nathan took them out in the car. He would ask them if they wanted to go anywhere or see anything, and sometimes they would point in a Ohio Tourbook that he gave them. They would point to stuff and he would take them there, like stuff downtown, buildings and stuff, and the airport, and a couple of historic churchs. There is one old historic church up the street. But they didn't go to that one.

Trouble is, there is not much to see in Ohio. There's some in Penneselvania. But not alot. I think. But I haven't spent that much time anywhere, so I should'nt say anything. I think Ohio is boring anyway. Nothing ever happens and there's nothing to do.

Until Zorg and Flez came.

Okay, I will tell you now about what was in the duffle bag. This happened, remember, a couple of weeks after they came to stay. Its' kind of hard to say what happened between that and when I found out about the duffel bag, except that it was summer, and we didn't do much. Nathan was still looking for a position. He's been looking for a position for a long time. He's always been looking for a position. That's what he calls a job. A position. He is a good motivator, and he likes people. He is a good communicator and has exceptional writing skills. At least that's what it says on his resume. That's French: resume. That's what our French teacher said. I'm taking French and it's hard. Resume should have that thing over the e that slants up, but I don't know how to do that character on this word processor. It's in the documentation but to hell with it.

Anyway, Nathan has been looking for a position as long as I've known him. He works sometimes, like I said, selling stuff. He tried insurance last year. That didn't work. He sold some insurance policies but not enough to make it worth while. The year before he worked as a public relations specialist at the University, but he had to drive too far everyday to commute, so he quit.

So that summer he wasn't working, but he was writing. He was always writing something. He says he could write a bestseller someday. But it won't be a novel, it will be more "autobiographical". I looked that word up. An autobiography is a biography written by yourself, about you.

"It will be about a journey of discovery" Nathan says.

"Discovering what" I asked?

"Myself", Nathan said. "An inner journey to discovery the real person behind the fassade that society forces me to put on. A journey by some inner road to the secret place that is me".

I sure as hell dont know what he means.

I guess I shouldnt' say hell or damn. But I see those words in books all the time. Brandon showed me all kinds of books with the F–word and everything. I didn't see any in Jack London or Robert A. Hienlein. I looked at the copywrite date in the Heinlen book and it said 1948. Wow that was a long time ago, and the Jack London book was even longer ago. They didn't have any swear words in them at all. Except I think "damn"! once in a while, but I don't remember. I wonder why newer books have the F–word and everything and they didn't have them back then? Maybe they didn't have the F–word back then.

But I was talking about what we did that summer. So, Mom worked, and Nathan looked for a position, I shot hoop's and Tyler went to day care three times a week to give Nathan a chance to work on his writing.

It happened one night. First, I have to tell you about the sounds in the night, coming from the ceiling.

Like someone was walking in the attic.

It's real scary sometimes, when that happens. Its happened before, sounds in the middle of the night like someone is walking up in the attic, but Mom told me that it's just the "house settling". It sounds scary, but I believe her. Just rafters creaking.

Well, I started hearing it again when Zorg and Flez moved in. Tiny footsteps upstairs in the attic. Nothing's up there, and in fact it's not much of an attic at all, just a crawlspace, in fact, and insulation. There are some boards across the joycets and we have boxes with old clothes in them up there.

It was creepy, hearing that. I would hear it just before I fell asleep and it would keep me from falling asleep. And then I'd hear other stuff, outside, crickets and those bugs in the trees that go buzz, and cars going down the street, and far away a tractor trailer blowing it's horn on the Interstate. Then a dog, and then two dogs.

Then the ceiling would creek again, and little feet would pitter patter across it. It was spooky.

Then I realized that the steps leading up to the attic trap door was in the spare bedroom.

Could Zorg and Flez be up there? Sure, I thought. Then it wasn't so creepy. But when I thought about it again, it was creepy again.

Oh, I also have to tell you that Zorg and Flez stopped eating with us. They just stayed up in thier room. Sometimes Mom would ask Nathan about it, and Nathan would say "Fruit. Their're vegetarians. I go out and buy fruit for them."

I never saw it. Still, Mom never asked about it. It was strange. Of course, the whole thing was strange. I didn't even think about it most of the time.

Anyway, this particular night, it was in August, and there were no noises coming from the attic that night, but there were noises coming from the spare bedroom and from the hallway. The door to my bedroom was closed and I could hear. Tyler was asleep. That kid sleeps like a log.

I listened. There was a bump against the wall between my bedroom and the spare one, and I listened some more. Then someone started walking down the hallway, and then I heard another bump, this one against the wall along the hallway. I listened more. I looked at the crack of light under the bedroom door. The light blinked out as someone passed. It sounded like they were dragging something.

Then, something went bump, bump, bump, down the stairs, only slow, not like it was falling. It was like bump —— bump —— bump —— like that.

I got up from the bed and went to the door. I put my hand on the doorknob and cracked the door open just a little. I looked out. I couldn't see anything. Who ever it was was almost all the way down the stairs to the living room.

I closed the door and went to the closet and got out a sweat shirt and pants, and I put my Reebok ahthletic shoes on real fast, went to the door, looked out, then went out and closed the door.

I passed Lori's room. She has her own room. I listened at her door. She doesn't snore but she breaths heavy. She was sleeping. That's not all she does in there. A couple of times shes had boys up there, when Mom and Nathan were away. One kid she had up, I remember him opening the door of her bedroom to go out to the bathroom, and I happened to be passing. I looked in and there was Lori in nothing but panties. Not that I thought she was anything great, but there she was, laying on the bed. Tell me they were'nt messing around!

She is not a slut or anything. At least I dont think so. But she likes boys.

I went downstairs into the dark living room. I looked around. I didn't see anybody. Then I heard the back door, the one off the kitchen, close softly.

So I went out to the kitchen, went to the window above

the sink, and looked out. I didn't see anything at first. But then I could see, because the moon was out and bright, that it was Zorg and Flez out there, going into the trees. They were carrying that big silver duffel bag.

I waited 'til they got into the underbrush, and then I opened the kitchen door quietly and slipped out.

It was cool, and the air was wet. A kind of fog was gliding along the ground, or a mist. Stars were out, and the moon was like a big shining face up there. It was quiet.

I followed them through the woods. On the other side there is a vacant lot with trees all around it. I stepped quietly, looking down because I didn't want to stumble or trip on something and maybe break a leg. I stepped over a log. Something hooted at me from a tree. I think it was a hoot, only it didn't sound like an owl. I was kind of nervous. It was spooky being out there at night, especially following these two goofy little guys.

Maybe they were taking off, leaving. I was kind of hoping that they were. But where were they going? Why didn't they just do out the front to the road? I couldn't figure it.

I couldn't figure where exactly they were going since there wasn't a bus stop near and there wasn't a train or anything they could take. They'd have to go into Keynesville. We live outside of Keynesville, if I haven't mentioned it, pretty far out into the boonies. It's a nice housing development, but like I said before it's boring.

Now I could see them out in the middle of the vacant lot. I stopped and hid behind a tree.

They were opening up the bag. How they did this I really couldn't see too good, but they got it open and it fell away flat on the ground. What had been inside looked like a big gray football, only shaped a little different. Hard to say what shape it was, except it was more like a football with some bulges in it. The two little guys looked it over for a minute, then they talked some, then they stepped back a ways from it, pretty far, while they were still looking at it.

I was looking at it too. I watched, and nothing happened for a while. At least I didn't think anything was happening, til I realized that the thing, whatever it was, was growing bigger very slowly. It swelled up like it was in a time-laps movie where everything is speeded up, like the kind you see where plants and flowers grow real fast. This looked like a squash growing, only not a pumpkin or an acorn squash, the kind Nathan makes us eat sometimes.

It got bigger and bigger, then it started getting REALLY big, like as big as a house, almost. It rose into the air as it grew.

I was impressed. I didn't know what it was supposed to be at first. I thought it was a balloon. But then something told me it wasn't. It began to flatten out on the bottom. It started looking more and more like a Frisbee with a bump on top.

A car passed on the road in front of the lot. There were trees along the road, pretty thick but if you were looking out the window of the car you might be able to see the thing, if you were looking up. Anyway, the car passed without even slowing down.

What was really strange, and when I started to get scared, was when parts of the big floating thing lit up and little lights flashed around on it. Like lights on an airplane but flashier. Now it looked like a ship, maybe a space ship, like in the movies. It looked real. It WAS real. I was looking right at it.

Then the thing stopped growing. It came down, slowly, almost until the underpart of the ship touched the tops of the tall weeds in the lot. Then it rose back up just a little bit.

Zorg and Flez walked toward the ship. They walked under it. Something opened up under there, a round hole, a hatch, I guess, and light came out from inside the ship. Zorg stood under the hatch, and then he rose right up into it. Then, after Flez picked up the duffel bag and folded it real neat and tucked it under his arm, he did the same thing, and the ship sucked him right up too. Just like that. It was real slick. No latters, no nothing. Just stand under that hole and up you go. I nearly fell over.

The hole closed. Lights started to flicker and dance all over the ship, and the whole under part of the ship glowed orange. Then it changed color to red. Then to blue. It was kind of neat, watching it. Then, real slow, it started to rise, wobbling a little, wavering in the air. It started slow, but by the time I got out from the trees to watch, it was practically gone, a little blinking light in the sky, like you couldn't tell if it was a plane or not.

I just stood there watching it for as long as I could, and it disappeared into the stars and was gone, like maybe into space. Where they had come from.

And I thought, so THAT's what they had in that silver duffel bag!

"Chapter Four"

I've been looking at books and stories. Novels, fiction, and stuff. And I think I'm still doing dialog wrong. Usually something comes after the "said". Like "He said loudly" and "she said softly" and like that. The punctuation is what gets me.

"I think this is the way you're supposed to do it," he said angrily.

"Yes, it surely is," she said languidly.

I think. Anyway, I'm copying it out of a book. I'll have to look up "languidly." But I don't have time now.

I wonder how semicolons work? You're supposed to put them between parts of a sentence; but I don't know what they'are for.

Anyway, after the spaceship left I stood there in the trees looking up at the stars. They weren't as bright as they are on nights when there's no moon, but as I told you, we're pretty far out in the country and they'are pretty bright by themselves.

They were winking and blinking a little. One of them looked red; if you looked at it for long enough.

And then, zzzzzip. I saw a shooting star; and it looked just like a star that had fallen, too; real fast. But it never hit the Earth, it just disappeared on it's way down. The flash it made was sort of greenish. I wondered if it had anything to do with the spaceship; but I guess not.

So I just stood there for a long time. How long it was, I dont know, I didn't have my watch. I don't wear it anyway much.

Then I got tired of standing there. I decided that they were not coming back, they had gone forever. I wasn't sad or anything. Like I said, they were strange. Not that I had anything against them. I just thought they were pretty wierd.

Wow, they were aliens, I thought. Then, when I thought about it somemore, it was not a big deal. I wondered about calling the police, but what would you say? Hello, this is Drew Hayes, and I just saw two aliens get in thier UFO and leave. They were staying with my family, in our house.

Uh huh. Yeah, right.

So, what could I do? I went back to the house and went upstairs and went to bed. Before I did I checked Mom's and Nathan's room. Nathan was snoring to beat all getout. He does that. Funny, Mom never wakes up. It keeps me up sometimes.

I went back to my room and closed the door and locked it. It was dumb to do, because the lock on the door isn't very good, like some alien would have a hard time getting in. But it made me feel a little better locking the door.

I took off my sweats and put my PJ's back on and got into bed. The ceiling was quiet. Nothing was moving up there. I thought about Zorg and Flez, and wondered what planet they came from. Mars or Pluto or someplace like that. Or maybe out even farther in the galaxy, like from a planet they have'nt discovered yet.

I wondered what kind of place it was, what color the sky was, if it was wierd or if it was pretty nice, like the Earth. What kind of food they ate, what they did for fun. That kind of stuff. I figured the place ought to be pretty different.

But I bet Zorg and Flez liked it. Maybe that's why they went back.

Boy, that was some neat spaceship. I guess thats what they call a "Flying Saucer" but it sort of looked different. It was curved differently. I can hardly discribe the neat way it curved. But the biggest thing that was like, real hard to understand was how it got bigger and smaller. I mean, that's real slick. It was like a balloon, and I couldn't figure it out. I didn't see them blow it up. There was no pump or some kind of air compresser. So how did they do it? I didn't have a clue, kid.

That was sure a funny spaceship.

I must have fallen asleep because when I got up it was morning and light was streaming through the window. I sat up real quick. Was it all a dream? Maybe I had dreamed it all, about Zorg and Flez and that crazy Flying Saucer!

I got out of bed and went out of the bedroom, and went to the door of the spare bedroom. The door was open a little. I pushed it open and looked in.

And there were Zorg and Flez asleep on the fouton, getting their Z's, just as peaceful as a lamb.

Boy, I didnt know what to think now. I was sure that wasn't a dream last night, but now I was thinking maybe it was.

Nathan came out into the hall. He looked in to Zorg and Flez's room.

Then he looked at me. "Anything wrong?" he said curiously.

"No," I said sadly. I shook my head.

"You look as if you have a problem," Nathan said loudly.

"No, I don't," I said quietly.

"You worried about the guys?" Nathan said concernedly.

"Nah," I said worriedly.

"Okay," Nathan said grinningly.

He went in to the bathroom.

I closed the bedroom door. Nope, I couldn't figure this

one out, unless they came back. I guess they did. But . . .

I opened the door again, and yeah, the big silver duffel bag was there, half sticking out of the closet.

I stood there, thinking about maybe trying to get that bag open by myself and getting a look at what was in it. But then I said to myself, you better not. Maybe the guys would get mad. And shoot me with a Fazier, like on Star Trek.

But I wasn't too worried about it. No, it wasn't a dream, I decided. I mean, it was too real. I didn't have to look into that silver duffel, I knew what was in it. A inflatible spaceship. A Flying Saucer you could blow up like it was a balloon.

Trouble was, nobody would ever believe me.

I didn't half believe it myself.

A couple of days past. Nothing much happened. It was August and school wasn't very far off. I was going into the 8th Grade. I wasn't very anxious to get back to school. It seemed like the summer just started. And this alien stuff was making it go real fast, though I don't know why.

One evening Mom was cooking, and she asked me to take the garbage out. I don't like to do that but I do it if she asks me. So I pulled the plastic bag out of the trash bin and looked for a twist-tie. I couldn't find one so I had to ask Mom, but she was busy and couldn't find one either, so I tried to tie the end of the bag off, only it was hard.

I dragged the bag outside to the trash cans. We have four trash cans, one for glass bottles and jars, one for plastic bottles and jars, one for paper, which goes to the municiple incinerater, and one for organic stuff, like coffee grounds and whatnot, but we never use that because we have a disposall in the sink. But the can is there anyway because the Township says you have to have it. I mean, I don't really think that a policeman is going to come up to the house and arrest everyone if we didn't have the forth can. But Nathan says we have to obey all "Green" laws and regulations, because we have to save the Earth. Okay, Nathan, if you say so.

Anyway, I dragged the bag out, which was mostly newpaper inside, and lifted it up to throw it in the can. It was sure heavy, and when I got it up the top came loose where I had tied it and half the stuff spilled out on to the ground. I swore.

I picked up the paper and packed the bag and tied it, and threw the bag in to the trash can. Then I saw that there was one more newspaper on the ground, and I picked it up. It was the front page of the Keynesville Chronicle, and I was about to just throw it in to the can, not bothering to open the bag again, when I saw "UFO." I looked at the article. The headline said UFO SIGHTED LOCALLY. The story was about how a UFO that was sighted in four different cities in the Midwest was seen in and around Keynesville too. People saw it all over. I read the article. I dont have it so I can't quote it, but it went on to tell about how this couple driving a car in Illinois saw it hoovering over them and they pulled off the road, just like we did! And a sherrif and his deputy in Indianapolis raced after the UFO and tried to intercept it. Boy was that dumb! How could you intercept a UFO? Anyway, they wrecked trying to do it, but nobody was hurt. Also, the Indianapolis Airport tracked it on radar, and so did a bunch of other airports. The article said the newspaper tried to contact the Air Force in Dayton, Ohio, but they didn't know anything about it.

I wondered if anything about this had been on the 6 O'Clock News. I never watch it myself, but maybe Nathan or Mom did. Maybe they saw it at 11 O'Clock.

I asked Mom about it.

"I've been too tired at night to watch the 11 O'Clock news," she said irritatedly.

"Oh," I said disappointedly.

"Why don't you call the TV station?" she said suggestively.

"What TV station?"

"Oh, try one in Dayton. Channel 6? I forget what broadcast stations there are since we've had cable. There are so many cable channels, I can't keep track of them."

"How do I find out what stations are in Dayton?"

"Call Information."

So I did. I just asked for the TV station in Dayton, and the operator said which one?, and I said any one, I didn't care.

The phone rang and some woman picked it up. I asked about the UFO, and they put me through to someone else. A man. I asked him about the UFO.

"Wait a second . . . Yeah, I think we did a silly season story on that two nights ago. Why, did you see it?"

"Uh, no," I said excitedly. "I didn't see it, exactly. But could you tell me about the story you put on the news?"

"Well, I don't have it up on the monitor right at the moment. What did you want to know?"

"I want to know what it looked like."

"What what looked like?"

"The UFO."

"Oh, I see. How old are you?"

"Thirteen. I'm doing a term paper in school about UFO's and I need to know what it looked like."

"School, huh? You going to summer school?"

Boy, that school story was a dumb thing to say! I thought. "Uh, yeah. Summer school. But I'm going to hand it in . . . at my regular school. You know?"

Man, was THAT lame, or what?

"Sure, kid. What's your name again?"

"Drew. Drew Hayes."

"Where do you live, Drew?"

I told him.

"Look," the guy said nicely, "I can send you a video cassette of the story we aired. Would that be okay?"

"Sure!"

"You have a VCR don't you?"

"Sure do!"

"Good, just give me your address and I'll send it off in today's mail."

So I gave him my address. Then I said thank you and hung up.

It came two days later. I ripped open the package and hurried to the VCR down in the game room. I put the cassette in and hit the PLAY button.

There was nothing. It was a reporter talking to the camera, standing out in the woods or something, and then he interviewed this farmer who saw the UFO. Only the farmer didn't see much, just some lights out in a field, and then in the morning he went out there and found this big bare spot on the ground, and a dead groundhog in the middle of it.

He also said he saw Bigfoot the week before.

Then the reporter interviewed some writer who lived near Keynesville. He wrote sci-fi. He was a guy with lots of wild hair and black glasses. His name was Trafford Starnes. The reporter asked him a few questions, and he answered, but he didn't say anything interesting. He didn't see the UFO. He didn't believe in UFO's, he said.

Great. Well, that was a big waste.

I wondered what the hell "silly season" was.

I guess your asking yourself by now what the heck Zorg and Flez were doing up there in thier room all the time, when they were'nt zooming around in thier Flying Saucer. Well, at first I don't know what they did, but as time went on, Nathan kept bringing them stuff. First he took the TV from the basement and gave it to them, and they watched TV alot. Then he even gave them the VCR, which I didn't want him to. They watched tapes.

I gave them my old Nintendo video game. Tyler said they could use his Sega game, but he never gave it up. He's going through the typically selfish stage.

So they sat in there and played video games, watched TV and tapes. They didn't read magazines or anything like that. I guess they couldn't read English. But they could speak it real good, sort of. That was odd.

They rarely came out, except when Nathan would drive them around. But after awhile they didn't even do that.

I wanted to tell somebody about this.

But there wasn't anybody. I think by this time, though, the neighbors were getting pretty suspicious. I saw Mrs. Carey across the street looking at them when Nathan and the guys went out to get in the car. I watched her from beside her house, which is next to Zabinski's. She looked real funny at those guys, let me tell you. Then she said something to someone inside, but I couldn't see who it was, but it might have been Mr. Carey, who is an alcoholic. They don't have any kids, but they have a nephew who comes to visit. He's a creep, though.

Anyway, there was just my friends, so I told Brandon Marscapone. I told him everything, about the UFO, and when the little guys came to live with us, and the spaceship in the vacant lot. Everything.

Brandon just looked at me.

"Yeah?" he said flatly.

"Yeah," I said affrimatively.

"That's really interesting."

"Yeah," I said noddingly. "So. Do you believe me?"

He shook his head. "No, I think your fibbing."

"But you've seen the little guys, didn't you?"

"Yeah. But they don't have no spaceship, I'll bet."

"They sure do!" I said shoutingly.

"Show me."

"How can I show you if they keep the spaceship up in their room?"

He laughed. "Up in their room," and he shook his head like he thought I was nuts.

Maybe I was nuts. Maybe I imagined the whole thing. Maybe I was taking drugs and having hallelucinations.

But I wasn't taking drugs. Then I must have been nuts.

As August went on and on, it was real hot, and the house was hot at night even with air conditioning. I could hear pitter patter with the little feet again, across the bedroom ceiling. I was getting pretty fed up with that.

Then one day Nathan went out in his old Van and came

back with a load of building stuff in it, like drywall and
spackling and lumber and stuff. And nails, and a bunch of
other junk, including a skylight. It was plastic and sort of
bubbleshaped, only kind of squared off. It was pretty big.

A skylight? For the attic? Yeah, that's what it was for,
because Nathan got his idea to finish the attic and make it
kind of a room for Zorg and Flez.

"They're kind of crowded in that bedroom," Nathan said
to Mom. "And we need the storage space."

"My God, Nathan, there's enough stuff here to finish it as
an apartment."

"Overhead's too low for normal people," Nathan said.
"But it's just right for Zorg and Flez."

Mom just looked at Nathan for a minute. Then she said,
"Nathan, how long are they going to be here?"

Nathan looked away. "Oh, I don't know. I keep meaning
to drive them to Dayton and let the Friends Committee
handle them."

"They won't turn them over to Immigration, will they?"

"Oh, no, God, that's not what they're for. They're for
support for people arriving in the country."

"Oh, good. So, when are they leaving?"

"I don't know, Cheryl. Soon, I hope."

But they didn't leave soon.

CHAPTER "5"

I've been reading more books, and I'm STILL having trouble with dialogue. It's not so easy.

I have too many he-said-somethinglyies.

You've got to mix them up a little. Like this—

"Oh, Fred, I love you," she husked.

"I love you too, Carol darling," he said lovingly.

"I want you, Fred, I need you," she snapped.

"Carol, I want to sleep with you and be your husband!" he shouted from the rooftops.

Like that. You have to put vareity in your writing.

One night, it was about a week from school starting, I heard all kinds of noises upstairs in the attic. There wasn't banging or anything, not like Nathan was still working up there. Just rustling and bustling and stuff.

I just laid there and listened. Boy, I was curious as to what the hell was going on. I mean, this was ridiculous. Here we had these wierd guys living with us, and they were obviously aliens, and nobody was interested, except for Mrs. Carey across the street. And Nathan and Mom and Tyler and Lori just slept like logs.

Lori didn't because she had a date almost every night. She would get home late, and I'd hear her, and usually when she opened the door to come in, the noise in the attic would stop. And Lori would come upstairs and go into her room, and in a little while the light would go out in her room, and then awhile later, the damn noises would start again, but Lori wouldn't here them. Was I the only one?

Jeez, this was getting decidedly tiresome.

"I'm going up there," I snapped to myself.

But I was a little afraid, so I took my time getting out of bed. I put my sweats on, and shoes, too, just in case they'd go out again. But they seemed like they were staying up there in the attic.

I was alone in the room that night because Tyler was staying with Grandma Alice in Columbus. She was my real Dad's mother. Grandma had drove up from Columbus and picked Tyler up. She's usually pretty nice to Tyler and Lori and me, Grandma Alice is. She isn't rich but she buys stuff for us alot. She's nice.

I opened the door to the bedroom and snuck out in to the hallway. I tip-toed to the spare bedroom. Lori wasn't home yet tonight, and I wanted to get up there before she came back.

But I was afraid. I mean, these guys were aliens. What would they do if they didn't want anyone watching them and they caught someone spying? They might zap me with thier Phazers. Or even worse.

But somehow, I wasn't all that afraid. I was scared, sure, but I wasn't like real scared, so that your tungue gets dry and tastes bad. That happened to me once, when I almost fell off a latter, when I went up it to get a ball off the roof. Never mind about that now.

I stood and put my ear against the door of the spare bedroom. The tv wasn't on, or the CD player of Nathan's that he gave them. Boy, he gave them everything. It was quiet in there.

They must of moved everything up to the attic, I thought. I was right.

I tried the doorknob. They never locked their door, I checked it now and then. The knob turned and I slowly opened the door, and looked in, and I saw that their futon wasn't there, or anything. The room was bare.

I came in and shut the door. The light was on, so I wasn't afraid. I went to the closet. Inside the closet, on one side, there are these big steps that go up to the attic, and there's a trap door at the top of the steps. The trap door was open. There were lights up there. I didn't hear any TV or CD player, but there was some noise, like birds or something. Actually, I knew what it was, it was them. The aliens. That's what they really sound like when their talking.

There were still some boxes of old clothse on the steps and on a shelf that ran along the wall. You had to squeeze past some of them. I creeped up the stairs. When I say big steps they are big, more like shelves than steps, if you get my meaning. Its hard to explain. But that's the way they built the house. There are only three steps, and you get to the trap door. So I kneeled down on the top step and listened.

More birds. I stayed that way, kneeling and listening, for a couple of minutes. Then I slowly raised my head til I could see over the edge of the hole.

There they were, Zorg and Flez, still dressed in slacks and Hawaaiin shirts, still looking a little like youknowwho. They weren't space aliens with anntennaes or anything. But something else was strange.

That skylight that Nathan had installed. It was pretty nifty. It could open.

And it was open.

Zorg and Flez were standing right under it, looking up and out, at the sky, I thought. Zorg began to raise his hands.

Suddenly, for no reason, because I wasn't making a sound, he turned his head and looked at me. He smiled.

Flez saw him, and turned in my direction. He looked a little surprised.

"Hey," Zorg said.

"Hey," I uttered.

"What are y'doin?" Zorg asked.

"Uh, what are YOU guys doin?" I stated.

Zorg giggled and so did Flez. They talked in bird talk for a while.

I stood up and looked around. Everything was up here all right, real cozy. And lots of other stuff that I didn't even know Nathan got them, boxes and cartons of stuff. I didn't look to see what it was exactly. It looked like video tapes and bunches of games and toys and stuff. Wow, some of it looked interesting.

Nathan had really fixed the place up, but it wasn't all finished. The drywall was up and spackled, but it wasn't sanded or painted yet. The floor was pine planks, but it didn't have varnish or anything on it yet. It was pretty nice little place to live, I guess, if you were four feet tall.

Zorg made a motion to come here. So I stepped up, and bumped my head against the slanting ceiling. I'm pretty tall for 13. I stooped and shuffled over to them.

Zorg raised his arm and pointed up, through the skylight. I edged over a little so I could look up.

I couldn't see anything, something was blocking the view. Then I thought, what the heck could be up there? So I put my head under the hole and straigted up.

Now I could see. I could see the roof and across the street, and all around, and I sure as heck could see what was floating above the house.

The Flying Saucer.

I stooped down again. "Neat!" I exclaimed.

Zorg giggled and shook his head. "Yeah, neat. You wanna go for a ride?"

Wow. I mean, that really hit me.

I swallowed before I said nervously, "You mean in the ship?"

"Yeah, we don't have a car," Flez said gigglingly.

"Nope, we don't," Zorg said jollyily. "We have a star-ship."

"COOL!" I said in a loud voice, but I hushed myself.

I didn't think about it too long, but I thought about it. I mean, what if they took off for space and never came back again? What if they took me to their planet and made me a slave or something, or a robot?

"Where are you going?" I asked.

"Just for a ride," Flez said.

"You're going to come back, right?"

Zorg nodded. "We like it here."

"And your not going to go back to your planet?"

"Not yet."

Both of them shook their big bald heads.

"You wouldn't like, do anything to me, would you?"

They shook their heads again, not smiling, like they're feelings were hurt or something.

"No. We like you. We want to have fun with you."

Zorg said that, and I looked at him. You know, for some silly damn reason I believed him. There was just something about him that you believed what he said. He was sincere. I cant explain it. Both of them were like that, Flez too.

"OK," I argued. "Let's go. Uh, what do we do?"

As soon as I said it the hole appeared in the bottom of the spaceship. Light poured out. It was bright, but not enough to hurt my eyes.

"What do I—"

But that's all I said before I just floated up. I mean, just floated, like I weighed practically nothing. Like I was on an elevator, only there was no elevator. I went up and through the hole and then to one side a little, and then I started to come down. My shoes touched the floor and there I was.

I was inside the alien spaceship.

And there was nothing to it. It was big and empty. The floor was soft, like soft plastic. It was just a big room, round, with a kind of dome in the middle, and that was it. The color was sort of greenish, but not too.

I walked around. Boy, there wasn't a stick of furniture, no instruments for the pilot, no nothing. Unless this was some kind of storage compartment and there were other compartments somewhere else. There were no seats to sit in, no shelves to put stuff up on, nowhere to hang anything. There was lots of nothing in that alien spaceship. I was kind of confused.

"Welcome," someone stated.

I didnt know who the heck it was. There was no one there.

"Make yourself comfortable," said the person who was saying that. I still did'nt see anyone.

"Hello!" I shuddered.

"Hello. You may call me Kel."

"Hello—Kel? Like, is that short for Kelly?"

"No. Please make yourself comfortable."

The floor started doing something funny, and it was sort of like what that robot did in that one Arnold Shcwartszenanager movie, it sort of flowed and came up and formed into something, and that something was a chair, sort of.

"Will this be usable?" Kel asked, but I still didn't see him. And I wasn't so sure it was a him. It wasn't a deep voice or a woman's voice either.

In fact, I was sure of something right away. Kel wasn't a regular person. He or she or it wasn't a human being. Well, neither were Zorg and Flez, but Kel was different from both of them too.

"Yeah, sure," I said.

"Please seat yourself."

I looked at the thing. Sure, I could sit down on it, though it was kind of curvy. So I did. I was kind of hard on my butt but I didn't say anything.

"Satisfactory?" Kel asked hospitalitly.

"Uh, yeah. Good. Fine." Like, what the heck was this place? It didn't make any sense.

"Will you be needing refreshment?"

"Huh?" I wondered.

"Would you like something to eat or drink?"

"Uh, nothing for me, thanks!" I said surprisedly. I wasn't expecting that.

"You're quite sure?"

"Uh. . . . . . . Uh. . . .OK. I'll have a Coke."

"With ice or without?"

"With, please."

"Very good."

The floor did the weird thing again, it started to get wavy and bulgy, and then a little table formed and came up, and on the table was this glass of Coke with ice.

I took it and looked at it. It felt cold. I smelled it. It smelled like Coke. I drank some. It tasted exactly like what it was supposed to taste like.

"Satisfactory?" asked Kel.

"Yeah, cool."

I was sort of like, I didn't know what to say about any of this.

I looked around and saw that Zorg and Flez were already in the ship, and there was no hole in the floor anymore.

"OK," Zorg said, "let's flarn."

Flarn? I was sure that's what he said. Flarn. OK, like, what the heck is that?

I didn't ask. I just sat there drinking my Coke. The boys sat in the middle of the floor and the floor got bumpy and puffed up, making a bunch of pillows. The guys sat among them with their legs crossed and their backs to one another, looking toward the walls.

I didn't understand why until the walls sort of dissolved, in spots, so you could see through them.

And WOW! We were flying. Just like that. And I didn't even know it until I looked. There was no way you could tell. There were no bumps or any feeling of motion. It was night and all you could see was lights, but you could see highways and shopping malls and house lights and everything. We must have been thousands of feet in the air already. It was just like being on a plane but not as bumpy.

And there was no noise at all. That was the spooky thing.

I watched cars crawl along the highway below. They looked like little toy cars with little battery-operated head-lights. The rows and rows of houses looked like model train villages under a Xmas tree, little windows all lighted up. I expected to see a pile of presents next.

We were over Columbus, I thought, not out in the country. We must have been moving real fast, because it takes like 30 minutes to get into Columbus from where we live. But here we were flying over it, and then we passed it, and went back out over empty areas again.

Here and there something lit up on the ground went by, or we went by it. Like a power station or something. It was pretty dark, not like when I saw the guys the first time flying their ship, with the moon up and all. There was no moon. Still there was a lot of light for it being night. I guess there's so much light at night now, with all the electric lights in the stores and homes and stuff. I read where astronomers have trouble keeping the city lights out of their telescopes, which is why they have to put them up on mountains out in the desert. But I wasn't thinking about that, I was sitting there enjoying the view.

The ship started to go down, and it didn't do it slow. It kind of swooped. But it didn't feel like a rollercoaster or anything. I wasn't getting motion sick, like I used to in the car sometimes when I was a little kid. It was smooth. We dipped and we were close to the ground. Funny thing was, when the ship turned or dipped or made any motion, it was the horizon that tilted, not us. Sort of like in a plane, you get the same effect sometimes, when the plane banks real hard, and I guess its the gravity that makes you stick to your seat. But this was a little different. You felt no sensation of movement, but a bit, and the ground went crazy out there. It was odd.

It was kind of dark down there except for a road, and the

only reason I knew there was a road was because we were following a car, one car. It was going along at a pretty good clip, its high beams on. Overhanging trees would hide it for a stretch, and then you could see it again. We were skimming along the tops of the trees, real close.

The reason we could see straight down was that part of the floor was like glass now. You could see straight through. Sort of a wedge shaped area.

We followed the car for a good stretch, and I was wondering why we were doing it, when I realized that now the ship was doing to this car and the people in it exactly what it did to our car and us.

The people or the driver in the car seemed to realize this as soon as I did, I mean, that something was following him. He or maybe it was she, started to swerve a little, and slow down. The ship slowed down to, then the car suddenly screeched and pulled off the road and stopped just like we did that night we saw the UFO.

Wow, this was really strange, to be up here in the ship instead of down there in the car, scared. I wasn't scared, but I was feeling pretty qeesy. I was getting a wierd feeling. Those people down there were probably scared.

But then again, it was kind of fun doing this. Like, you know, playing ticktack at Holloween, throwing pebbles at peoples windows, or papering their trees. That means hanging toilet paper all over the branches, if youve never seen it. Or had it done.

It was fun. The ship swooped, turned, and then came back, and then it slowed and stopped, right above the car.

Then it lowered until it was right above the car, and I could hear some people talking. They were in the car.

"What is it? Oh, my God, Carl, what is it!"

"Jeeez!!! I don't know!!!"

"Tell it to go away, Carl!!!"

"You tell 'em!!!"

"Carl, I feel sick!!!!!"

"Don't throw up on the leather!!!"

"Ohhhhhhhhhh!!!!!"

The guy stuck his arm out the window and waved it real fast.

"Hey, get the F out of here!!! Leave us alone!!!!!"

He used the F word. He was like more mad than scared, but he was pretty scared too.

Then, suddenly, the ship lifted and we sailed away, real fast.

We gain altitude again and cruised over cities and towns. More highways with little toy cars, smaller this time, because I guess we were really high.

We passed through clouds and it was like fog, yet you could still see the ground, only it turned a different color. Like red or something. I didn't get that. Anyway, we flew faster and higher, and it was really neat.

There was something out there, flashing. It looked pretty wierd and I wondered what it was. It had flashing lights all over it and it was flying. It was bobbing up and down, so it couldn't of been a plane.

But I was fooled, because it was a plane, an airline plane, a 747 or some big jet. The reason it was bobbing wasn't because it was, it was the ship, I guess. I told you you couldn't tell if the ship was moving or doing any movements. Well, the ship settled down and now I could see it was a jet. You could see the windows all lighted up. There were numbers on it and it had the name of the airline, but I forget what it read, it was one of them like American or something. You couldn't really see it all that good. And there were lights blinking all over the plane. We were behind it, then we came alongside, and then we pulled ahead. Then we dropped and it flew over us, and you could see it against the stars.

It was neat that different parts of the floor and walls and ceiling in the ship could become transparent so you could see, depending on where what you wanted to see was at the time.

Then we rose again, and came up alongside the plane, and

we got real close, like you could look right in the windows. I saw some faces. Not everybody was looking. Just a few people. I thought somebody waved, but I'm not sure.

We flew like that beside it for awhile, then I guess Zorg and Flez got tired of it, and the ship zoomed away, and that plane got tiny in a second, and in another second it was GONE.

Wow, could that spaceship fly fast or what.

Chapter 'SIX'

I finally fixed my Spellchecker!! It was in the wrong Directory on the Hard Disk. I moved it, and now it works. It's real slick. I corrected the spelling on a couple of chapters and BOY, was it bad. I mean, the worst. I can't spell for sour dog poop. Now I'll be the best speller in the world. Well, maybe not that good, because I still get things confused a bit.

I didn't print out the corrected chapters, because my printer is on the blink. Besides, I might not have saved those files right. But never mind.

Also, I found another program in the stuff the computer came with. It's called Editech, and it sort of goes over what you write and tells you when you've made a boo-boo. It's really great! It corrects grammar, punctuation, and everything! My writing is a lot better now that I have those two programs working. Maybe one day I will be published. You never know.

Dialogue is still a problem, and they don't make a computer program to help you with that, or at least I don't think they do. I think I'm doing it better, though. I think the problem could be all the "ly" words, like tiredly and worriedly. I can't even find "tiredly" in the Dictionary. So I won't used it, even if I did before, which I can't remember. You really don't need a lot of "saids" either. Or any of those words that substitute.

"Get out!" he barked.

See, it works, but if you have too many of those, everybody barking and snapping and hissing all over the page, then it's kind of silly. I've even read books that have too much of this. I didn't realize that you could publish something that's pretty bad.

It seemed like we were flying in space now. The stars were bright. I didn't know how high we were.

"Are you comfortable and in good spirits?"

It was Kel that said that.

I said, "Yeah, sure. Hey, uh . . ."

"Is there something I can do for you?"

"Yeah, Kel. You could answer some questions, maybe."

"Of course. What do you wish to know?"

"Like, who's steering the ship?"

"Do you mean who is in command? My masters are."

"Masters?"

"Yes. Your hosts."

"Zorg and Flez?"

"Correct."

"Oh. But they're just sitting there watching."

"Nevertheless, they are commanding the ship."

"Uh-huh. Mm, what do you do, Kel?"

"I am the ship."

"Oh."

That made sense. I didn't know how, but it did.

Kel seemed to think I was confused. "Perhaps I should qualify. I contain many automatic mechanisms, and these mechanisms, in a sense, control all aspects of the space-craft's operations. My masters do not actually pilot the ship, but they do command it. Have I made myself more clear?"

"Sure, I understand," I said, nodding.

"May I refresh your drink?"

"Huh? Oh, sure, yeah."

Kel refreshed my drink. The table sank, gurgled, rose again, and there was a full glass on it, with more ice. Awesome.

Everything was awesome about this ship. I was having a good old time! I watched the stars. They didn't move, except when the ship turned. It wasn't like the Enterprise, with the stars shooting by. There were lots of them. I had never seen so many stars. I guess there were planets up there, like Mars and Jupiter, but I couldn't tell which ones they were. I read a few astronomy books once. It was interesting. I wondered if you could see any satellites from here. Like, the Russian Space Station, or the TV satellites, or something like that.

I looked down again. Something was happening. The lights were stopping, and there was this huge dark area moving below. The lights just stopped in a line going off sideways to the way we were flying. It was a jagged line. And along it I thought I saw, like, light reflecting.

It was the sea down there. OK, that made sense, we were going over the ocean. Cool, I thought. But where the heck are we going? I didn't want to get too far away from home, right? I mean, if Mom would wake up and look in my room and see me gone, she would get real worried. Heck, she'd throw a fit. Have a kitten.

But then I remembered that when Zorg and Flez went out before, they came back before morning. So then I wasn't too worried about it. They promised to take me back. Didn't they?

I watched the ocean. Which was nothing but darkness, except every once in a while you could see some lights, tiny ones, down there floating around. Boats I guess. Anyway there wasn't much to look at, so I looked at the stars again, and when I looked down a little later, there were lights.

Man, we'd crossed that ocean in a hurry. I wondered what

the heck ocean it was, the Atlantic or the Pacific. I wished I knew the stars well enough to navigate.

We flew. This was another country. I had never been to another country before except Mexico. Canada doesn't count, even though they have colored money. OK, our money is colored but it's a dull green. Canadian money is pretty, and there's a picture of the Queen of England on it, which I don't understand, because I thought Canada was a separate country.

"Kel, what country is this?"

"This is Ireland. We will be in Great Britain . . . we have entered Great Britain. We are now overflying Wales."

Wales didn't look any different than Ireland. But then, you really couldn't see much except an occasional light. I'm sure Wales and Ireland look different in daylight.

Pretty soon Kel said, "We are now in England."

It was dark down there as the ship lost altitude fast. We swooped like a bird. I looked out through the walls. It looked like we were over farms and fields and that stuff. The wheat or whatever it was, was tall.

"Zorg?"

Zorg turned his bald head to me. "Yeah, Drew?"

"What are we doing in England?"

"Going to have a little fun. Make some circles."

I nodded. "Right. Gotcha."

Boy, I didn't have the slightest idea of what the heck he was talking about. But I found out.

The ship stopped out in the middle of a field somewhere. It was dark as hell, but for some reason I could see out there. It was like looking through a Night-Scope, like the kind the Army used in the Golf War. The wheat or whatever was tall and dry looking and kind of light brown. It was moving slowly, very slowly in the night wind. I was wondering what the heck we were doing.

Zorg and Flez were looking toward a spot on the wall, and something was on the wall, a figure made up of circles. Then it changed to another figure. Then another. Zorg and

Flez were looking at these, as if they were deciding something. Zorg chirped something, and the figure changed again. This one had lots of little circles connected by lines and things. Flez made like a bird, then they both cheebled and sang. They started giggling.

The floor got transparent, and I looked down. It was strange. The wheat was sort of laying over, like in waves going around in circles. It made a big circle, then the ship moved and another circle started, then a third circle, and then it was done.

The ship rose a little, and we all looked down.

It was a bunch of circles in wheat. All the wheat was pressed down. It wasn't cut. It was just bent over and kind of mashed.

"What the hell?" I said.

Zorg and Flez were laughing like it was the funniest thing they ever saw.

I didn't get it.

But on second thought, it looked like fun. Maybe.

The ship started moving again, flying over the fields. It buzzed like a farmhouse, then took off for the sky again.

The ship kept flitting around, and every once in a while it would get close to a house or something. A couple of times nothing happened. But once, when the ship got really close to this, like, white-colored cottage, the lights came on and this old guy came out of the front door carrying a gun. It looked like a shotgun. He pointed it at the ship.

"Whoa!" I said, but I didn't move. I was kind of startled. Sort of frozen to the chair.

BLAM!

Wow, the guy let loose with both barrels.

Zorg and Flez fell on the floor laughing. Then I started to laugh. It was pretty funny, if you thought about it. There was this scrawny guy in baggy underwear, shooting at us. He looked so silly. I mean, was this guy lame or what. Did he think he was going to bag a Flying Saucer? The guy was a moron. Why didn't he just wave or something? I guess he never thought he might be starting a space war by doing that, taking potshots at aliens. What a jerk.

Some people have no consideration.

So, anyway, I started to have a good time. We zipped over here and over there, and I think we got near London once—actually I'm only guessing. I didn't see Big Ben or Buckingham Palace or anything. It was just a big city. It could have been Liverpool, for all I knew. I didn't bother to ask Kel where we were, because I was having such a good time zooming around, dodging and diving and scaring the heck out of people. Not that we did anything bad. We didn't do anything bad. Just had a good time.

We made a couple of more wheat circles, and it was fun. I really enjoyed it, even though it was a little dumb.

Then, somehow, I guess I was feeling my oats or whatever, but I got this idea.

"Zorg?"

"Yeah, Drew?"

"Can we go into space?"

"Sure, if you want to. I thought you didn't want to."

"Yeah, but I do now."

"Okay. Let's go."

And did we go. The ship turned upward and ZOOOOOOM! Man, we shot towards the sky like a rocket. Heck, this was better than any rocket. I mean, the Space Shuttle doesn't go that fast.

We rose high, high above the Earth. What a view! It was awesome. You could see the curve of the Earth real good, even in the dark. I looked down through the floor. Cities were like diamonds scattered all over, glittering and blinking, and thin strings of lights connected all the cities up, like it was all one big spider web lit up like a Xmas tree in the darkness.

And there wasn't a sound, either. Nothing. But we'd been able to hear the shotgun go off, and people talking, and everything. I keep mentioning it, but, well, it was really weird.

Then something really really weird happened. The sun came up. That's what I said, because we were coming over the curve of the Earth, going towards it. The sun rose and it was big and fiery. But for some reason I could look right at it. It was sort of partially blocked out, or something. I didn't quite understand that, because usually, as you know, you can't look directly at the sun.

We veered off and the earth swung away. I still watched it. I couldn't take my eyes off it. It was big, a huge blue and white ball with clouds streaming all over it. And here and there some brown stuff, and I knew that was the land, the continents, all spread out like a map, except it was hard to recognize things. I thought I saw China or something big. Anyway, it was really neat seeing it like this. I mean, it was more than neat. I was thinking, everything is on that globe. Every person, every human being alive. And everything that is in the world is there. That's it, that's the whole ball of wax. That's everything. I couldn't get over it. We live there, we, everybody. All human beings. This is all we have and we've got to live there. And we have to get along with each other because if we don't, there's no place else to go. For now.

For now. Wow. Then I started thinking . . . hey, what if the Earth isn't all we have? Huh? What if . . .

Whew! I didn't want to start thinking about such heavy things. This was all too awesome for me.

I looked at the Earth again. It was shrinking as we got farther away from it. It looked like a blue marble now and it had this big shiny spot on it where the sunlight hit it. Man, it was terrific, looking out and seeing the whole Earth like that.

I laughed. I don't know why, but I was so whelmed over.

Zorg looked at me. He was smiling and giggling a little bit. "You having a good time, Drew?"

"Yeah, sure!" I said. I sure was.

"Want to get stupid?"

"Huh?"

He held out his hand. There were little white things in it. It looked like some pills.

"Take these, you'll enjoy it even more."

He dumped them in my hand. They were pills all right. I didn't feel good about taking them. I mean, they warn you so much about taking drugs. This is your brain on drugs, and there's this egg frying in a pan. I get the message. They say there's drugs in the schools but no one I know has any drugs at our school. Unless you count Jason Benedetto. He drinks beer out of his dad's bar refrigerator. He gets drunk. He asked me to come over and get drunk once, but I didn't.

Anyway, I was kind of worried about taking the stuff.

"Kel, what are these?"

"Neurological effectuators," Kel told me.

"Yeah. What is that?"

"Those particular ones lower higher-level cerebral functioning while increasing receptivity of the brain's pleasure centers. My masters take them regularly to increase enjoyment and relax inhibitions. They are completely harmless, and the effects are temporary."

"Will they work on me?" I asked.

"The sub-microscopic molecular computers contained in the drug can adapt to any generally humanoid life form, yours included. However, I can't predict how long they will take to do their work. It may be quite some time. On individuals of my masters' species, the effects come within hours. With you, the process might take much longer."

"How much longer? Days? Weeks?"

"Days, surely. Perhaps a few weeks at the outside."

"Huh-huh. Thanks."

I wasn't sure I understood all that. I looked at the pills. They were normal size and looked like you wouldn't choke on them.

I didn't want to take them.

"I don't want to take these," I said.

"You don't have to," Zorg said. "If you don't want to."

"Thanks, but no thanks," I said. "I don't want to be stupid. I'd rather be smart."

"Oh." Zorg reached for what was on another table that was coming out of the floor. More pills.

"Here, take these, then," he said, handing me more pills. "If you want to be smart."

These new ones were yellow. I put the white ones in my pocket.

"How smart will they make me?" I took the yellow ones from him.

"As smart as you want to be," Zorg said. "Real smart, if you want."

"I want to be pretty smart. Sometimes I think I'm not so smart. How many pills should I take?"

Zorg shrugged. "Take, maybe, three. Then take one a day until you're as smart as you want."

"Okay." So I popped three of the pills into my mouth and washed them down with Coke.

"I hope they don't make me sick," I said. I was a little worried about it.

"Don't worry, they're safe," Zorg said.

I sure hoped they were. I wondered if this was all part of "flarning," whatever the heck that was.

Chapter 7

I've been reading more lately. I read a whole book last night before I went to bed. I've never done that before. It was an interesting book, but a little hard to read. It was *The Sun Also Rises* by Ernest Hemingway. I kind of liked it, especially about Spain and the bullfights, though I bet Nathan would have a thing to say about bullfights and how nasty they are, from an animal rights point of view. He went on a demonstration once against using animals for experiments. He didn't get arrested. He goes on demonstrations a lot. I guess he's committed and has sensitivity. Nathan is a good guy. But anyway, the Hemingway book was his. I got it from his bookcase. Goes to show you something. Don't know exactly what.

A couple of minutes after I took the yellow pills, we reached the Moon.

Yeah.

That's what I said. We went to the Moon. Now, this about floored me. I never thought I'd go to the Moon. I used to think I might want to be an astronaut, but now they're cutting the Space Budget, and, well, you can just about forget about the Space Program. It's history. It's in the archives, dude.

But here I was, going to the Moon. It was nothing less than fantastic.

I looked down. The moon's bumpy surface spread out like the face of some kid with bad acne. There were millions of craters, and there were mountains, and valleys and all sorts of curvy canyons and stuff. It was neat looking at it close up. It looked just like the picture the astronauts took, but this was real. It was so real.

We headed for the surface so fast I thought we were going to crash. But at the last second, it seemed, we slowed and began gliding like a Frisbee over smooth hills and wide craters. Our height was no more than a thousand feet, I guessed, but it was just a guess.

The Moon's color is this really light gray. It's very bright and reflects a lot. I guess that's why the moon shines so much. You could see everything clearly. The closer you got the more craters you could see. There were craters everywhere, even little ones a couple of yards across. Where there weren't craters there were piles of rocks. Rocks were all over the place, big ones, little ones, jagged ones, smooth ones. And everything was covered over with a coating of light gray dust, like the stuff you find under the bed. Dust Bunnies on the Moon!

We slowed down and started hovering over one spot. I looked to my right and I could see something that wasn't natural. By that I mean, it couldn't have been part of the moon. It was a bunch of junk, and someone had left it there.

"Your people have been here," Flez said, smiling. "See?"

I saw. It had to be one of the places that the astronauts had landed!

Wow, this topped everything. This was the actual place that they had landed. I wondered which Apollo mission it was, the first one maybe. But I had no way of knowing. I didn't know what part of the Moon we were in, and I couldn't remember where the first Apollo astronauts had

come down. The Sea of Something or Other. Well, anyway,
whether or not it was the first Moon Landing place, it was
really neat to be there.

"Do you want to go out and walk around?" Zorg asked.

"Huh?" I was floored by that.

"You know, go outside the ship?"

"Holy cow! Uh, don't I need a space suit?"

"We can give you one," Zorg said.

What *couldn't* these guys do?

"Okay," I said. "Sure. Yeah, I'd like to try that."

Well, I did it. It's kind of hard to explain how, but here's
what happened.

Kel told me to stand on a spot on the floor. And the floor
opened, and I could see the ground, or the surface, whatever
you call it. It wasn't very far down. The strange thing was
that I didn't fall. I thought I was going to fall, but I didn't,
not right away. I sort of floated down.

Now, I wasn't wearing any space suit. What was around
me was some kind of bubble. I knew it was there, because
I could feel it. It was kind of prickly. It was like being inside
an invisible balloon, but I could walk around once I got used
to it.

I walked around, bouncing into the "air." (There isn't any
air on the Moon.) I was as light as a feather. I could almost
float. And when I touched down, I left no footprints. That
was really weird. Try as hard as I could, I couldn't leave any
footprints in the dust.

There were lots of footprints around, from the astronauts.
And junk. There was more junk there than in a junk yard.
All kinds of complex stuff, with antennas and screens and
sheets of plastic. There were boxes and sacks and even a
bottle or two, though not made of glass.

Those guys really littered up the place! I guess back then,
back in the 1950s—You know, I forget the date that they
landed on the Moon—Well, whenever it was, they probably
didn't have Ecology. I guess they didn't know they were
messing up the environment. If they'd have tried to go

today, the Ecology people probably would have stopped them, with demonstrations and stuff. Or maybe Congress would have passed a law that they couldn't go.

I don't know, though, it would have been a shame if that had happened. Even though they trashed the Moon, it's really a great accomplishment that they went there. I've always wondered why they never went back. I mean, they spent all that money, and they did it, and then they quit. How come they didn't build a hotel or something here? You could charge a lot of money and people would probably pay it to come here. Oh, well.

I spent some time bouncing around, looking at things. I looked up at the Earth. It was as beautiful as ever, though it was far, far away. I got homesick just looking at it.

Then I got bored and went back to the ship. Kel floated me up into it, and the door in the floor closed. The prickly envelope around me disappeared.

"Hey, that was neat!" I said.

"You enjoyed it?" Flez asked.

"Yeah. I mean, it was okay. Cool."

"Cool," Zorg said, nodding and giggling.

Then something happened, but I didn't know exactly what at the time. Zorg and Flez stopped smiling and kind of looked at each other funny.

I watched them, wondering what was going on. Suddenly they looked worried.

They sat back down as the ship zoomed away from the landing spot, shooting across the lunar terrain. I still didn't feel any motion, but it made me kind of dizzy to look out at everything zipping past. Sheesh, we were really moving at a good clip.

Then, we screeched to a stop and dropped into a huge crater. We went all the way down, and then the ship did a strange thing. It touched the surface and landed with a soft bump, and then it buried itself in the dust. It sort of rotated back and forth for a while until the dust partially covered it.

Then everything in the ship kind of turned off. The lights

went out. It was mostly dark, except for a faint light coming from the ceiling.

"What are we doing?" I asked.

"Hiding," Zorg said, and he was worried.

"From who?"

"Blog."

"Blog, huh?"

"Yeah, Blog is a real drag," Flez said. "If he catches us, it'll be pretty bad."

"Oh."

Jeez, that sort of worried me, too. Blog. The name didn't sound too good, just by itself.

"What did you do that Blog is after you for?"

"Drew, we have to be quiet now," Flez said. "Real quiet."

"Oh. Sure, yeah."

Whew! So, I just sat there. We sat there for a long time, but maybe it only seemed like a long time. Zorg and Flez didn't say anything, and I sure didn't. Neither did Kel. Maybe he was shut off.

You could hear a pin drop in that ship. I sweated a little. It was getting pretty hot in there. I wondered about that. Shouldn't it have been getting cold? I mean, it's supposed to be cold in space. Oh, well, it didn't matter. It didn't get too hot.

Finally, the lights came back on and Zorg and Flez starting smiling again.

"We can start having fun again," Zorg said.

"Great!" I said. I was relieved to hear it.

So, we returned to Earth. The trip back was even faster, or maybe it just seemed like it. I figured it was nearly morning, and I had to get back. I asked Zorg if we were going to go back right away, and he said sure thing.

The Earth got bigger and bigger, and it got all beautiful all over again, even more, as we headed for the night side. The cities came up again like diamonds scattered across the darkness, one after another.

The ship lost altitude fast.

Then, from the right came something. It was a jet, a military jet. I could see, though it was rather far away. Must have been magnified or something. It was an F-16, I think. Anyway, it was heading for us like a bat out of hell. It chased us, then it caught up with us and pulled alongside.

This was exciting, or rather scary, too. Now the Air Force was after us. Of course, I would rather have the US Air Force catch us than "Blog," whoever or whatever that was.

Then again, the Air Force might shoot us down. I suddenly got kind of scared that that would happen.

Then I heard the jet's pilot talk to us. He was telling us to identify ourselves.

Flez and Zorg were giggling like crazy.

"Hey, guys, maybe we should pull over?" I suggested.

They giggled at that, too.

The pilot kept talking, repeating orders to identify ourselves, and that we were violating United States airspace.

Well, we flew like that for a while, with the jet pacing us and the pilot jabbering away. Then, another jet approached, another military jet. And I think there were more coming at us from farther away.

So we got out of there. I mean, we REALLY took off this time, WHOOOSH!!!

Those jets were like gone in a second, left in the dust.

Cool.

We went home. No more Air Force jets gave us any trouble. Next thing I knew, our street was below, and then our house. The ship hovered just above the skylight.

The skylight was open. I dropped from the ship right through it, and there I was, back in the attic.

Zorg and Flez followed. Then something really weird happened. The ship shrank. Yup, it did. It was amazing to watch. It shrank to the size of a football, just like before, and it dropped right through the skylight. Zorg closed the skylight and locked it. The ship floated to the floor. Then

Flez held the duffel open and Zorg slipped it in. It fit right in, just as slick as you please.

I asked Zorg how they could do that, and he told me the ship was made of ultrathin material that was ultralight, too. More than that, the stuff wasn't like ordinary matter. It had more space in it between atoms and molecules, if you follow. Like, four times as much space, and it could adjust its own molecular structure and become more dense. Does that make sense? Well, that's the way it worked. I asked about the weight. I mean, even if it shrank, it would weigh a ton.

And Zorg said, "Well, doesn't it float?"

"Huh? You mean the ship?"

"Doesn't it float by itself?"

"Sure."

"Well, we don't turn the ship off when we shrink it."

"Oh. I get it."

So that's how it was done.

And that's what a flarn is. Flarning is fun. A little dangerous sometimes, but that makes it more fun, I think.

Chapter 8

I read *The Count of Monte Cristo* last night. It was good. Reading is getting easier, for some reason. Today I'm reading *The Grapes of Wrath* by John Steinbeck. There's another Steinbeck title on the shelf, *East of Eden*, and I'll probably read that, too. Good thing Nathan has a lot of books, because I'm getting into this reading thing.

I showed some more of this material to Mr. Olander. He was impressed.

"Drew, this *is* fiction you're writing, isn't it?"

I nodded. "Yeah, sure."

He looked relieved. "You had me worried. I was about to send you to the counselor."

"Why? Would I be crazy if it was true?"

He chuckled. "Good question. Anyway, it's pretty good, this stuff, for your age. You might have the makings of a real writer. Your spelling is improving by leaps and bounds."

"Thanks."

Well, I couldn't take credit for that, could I? But I did. I couldn't tell him my writing was machine-laundered.

"Where did you get the idea to use yourself as a character?"

I shrugged. "Oh, I don't know. It just came to me."

"That's very innovative, you know. Very . . . post-modern."

"Uh-huh. What's that mean?"

Mr. Olander looked stumped. "You know, the word's bandied about so much . . . Never mind. Very good, Drew. Keep it up."

"Sure. Thanks, Mr. Olander."

I didn't go out flarning with Zorg and Flez again before school started. They didn't flarn all that much, maybe twice a month, if that. They did take me again about a week after Labor Day, but nothing much happened that night. We made some circles in a hayfield, but it didn't make the papers or anything. "Crop circles" is I guess what you properly call them. I've been reading about them. They seem to crop up (pun?) in England a lot, but they're turning up here regularly now. I can't believe it's Zorg and Flez doing all that. I've tried to ask them about other aliens and they nod their heads, but don't say much.

Nor are they very talkative on the subject of Blog, who, incidentally, didn't show up the second time we flarned. I sure am curious as to what Blog could be, but Z. And F. aren't saying. Oh, well, I gather the little guys are in trouble with this Blog character. Blog may be some kind of alien policeman. Policeperson? But I'm just guessing. Blog could be a monster that's after them. Sounds like it. Or just someone . . . some creature whose out for revenge.

Ooops, that should be "who's out for revenge." I left that in to show that I still get confused, but at least I'm catching my errors now. Some of them. English isn't an easy language. Take French . . . please!

That's just a joke. Actually, French is getting easier this year. I don't know why. In fact, I'm doing fairly well in all my subjects so far.

Maybe those smart pills are working. I don't know, it's been weeks since I took them, and I really haven't noticed anything radically different. I don't feel very smart. I haven't figured anything out yet, about Zorg and Flez, or about anything important. Smart people are supposed to figure things out, aren't they?

Okay, I should tell you about the tabloid reporter who came snooping around here. He started things off.

You know what the tabloids are: those goofy-looking newspapers that you see in the racks by the check-out counters in the supermarket; the ones with the color pictures of Elvis Presley, who's supposedly still alive somewhere, walking around big as life—bigger, since he gained all that weight; and stories about how Bigfoot got this guy's wife pregnant, and about what movie stars are sleeping with what other movie stars. That sort of stuff. Gossip. Trash. Silly stuff. And they always have stories about UFO's and aliens and strange goings-on.

It was right before Labor Day. Mom was working, Lori was out with a bunch of boys who had driven up to the house in a fancy sports car, Tyler was at Grandma Peg's (Mom's mom), and Nathan was out. I was reading *Scaramouche* by Raphael Sabatini. It was kind of purplish, prosewise, but fun.

The doorbell rang and I reluctantly put down the book and went to answer it.

The guy at the front door was on the short side and balding, but on the young side of forty, I'd say, dressed in khaki slacks and sport shirt, loafers, no socks. I think that's dumb. Your feet get stinky, but never mind.

"Hi! Is this the Hayes residence?"

"Yeah," I said warily.

His smile was friendly enough. "I'm Dick Chambers. Reporter for the World Gazette?"

He said it like a question. It didn't mean anything to me at the time. "Yeah?"

"You ever read the Gazette? Or your parents, maybe."

"No."

"Oh. Well, it's a newspaper. You've probably seen it at the supermarket."

"Uh-huh." I got kind of reticent when I don't know what a person's angle is.

"Anyway, I'd like to talk to your parents, if they're around."

"Nope."

He chuckled. "Nope, they're not around, or nope, I can't talk to them?"

"Nope, they're not around."

"Oh. Well, would you mind talking to me?"

"About what?"

I wasn't about to give this guy a break.

"About UFO's. What's your name, by the way?"

I told him. "What about UFO's?"

"Drew, your neighbors say there've been a lot of UFO's sighted around here lately."

"Yeah?"

"Yeah. Spotted any yourself?"

Uh-oh.

Well, I had some choices here. I could spill the beans about Zorg and Flez, or I could calm up. Another alternative was to string him along and see what he knew, then feed him bits of info, deciding as I went along what bits to offer.

I resolved to do the third thing.

"Really haven't *spotted* any flying saucers."

"No? Your friends and neighbors have been seeing quite a few of them. In fact, they claim your house has been the center of all the activity."

"They do, eh?"

"Yes, sir."

"That's interesting."

Chambers took out a notebook and a stubby pencil. "I'd say it was interesting. You don't mind if I take some notes, do you?"

"No, sure, go ahead."

"Uh, how about if I come in?"

"My parents don't let me admit strangers when I'm alone."

"Oh, yeah. Of course, sorry about that. Look, why don't we go out and talk in the yard? Would your folks have any problem with that?"

I thought about it. "That would probably be okay. I can run pretty fast."

He laughed. "I bet you can. Okay, come on out, then, if it's not too much trouble."

"No trouble."

I went out. It was a nice day, sunny and warm. Kids were playing on the street. The sky was pure blue. It was still summer, but something about the air, maybe the light, said fall was coming. Funny how things can be subtle like that.

He asked me how old I was and where I went to school and what grade and all that, and I told him.

"Drew, why do you think your neighbors are saying these things if they aren't true?"

"I didn't say they aren't true."

"You're not saying that? Really? Let me tell you, some of these stories are pretty wild."

I nodded. "Yeah? Like what, for instance?"

"Uh, for instance. Well, for instance, there's a kid down here . . . I have his name. Damon Zabriski?"

"Zabinski."

"Yeah, I can't read my own chicken scratches. Anyway, he says he saw a UFO right above your house. In fact, he says . . . and this is really pretty wild—he says it came *out* of your house. Somehow, though he wasn't specific. Can you tell me a little bit about that?"

"Pretty wild," I commented.

"Yeah. Is Damon just fibbing?"

"I've known him to fib a little."

"So, it's not true?"

"Didn't say that."

"Okay," he said simply as he jotted something down in his notebook.

I was curious as to what I'd said that rated getting written down. Beats me, I thought.

"So, you haven't really seen anything yourself, but . . ." He waited for me.

"Didn't say that either."

"Uh-*huh*."

This guy was a little weird himself. He sort of bit his tongue when he wrote, as if writing was really hard to do. Maybe it was.

"Listen, what your neighbors are saying, see, is that—"

"Yeah, I know, that aliens are living in our house."

"Ah."

"Yeah, and that they keep their flying saucer inside the house, because . . . well, they can do that because it's collapsible, you see."

"Collapsible? Really. A collapsible flying saucer."

He really liked that part, I could see.

"Yeah," I went on. "And they uncollapse it every once in a while and take off in it . . . you know."

"Yeah, yeah." Chambers was writing up a storm, there.

"And go off and do stuff. Then they come back."

"Right. And they live right in your house."

"I didn't say that."

He looked up from his notebook. "Right. So, where are these aliens from?"

"I don't know."

"They haven't told you?"

"Nobody told me anything."

He started scribbling again. "Good, good . . . uh-huh. So, you don't know the name of their planet?"

"I don't know about any planets."

"Good, good. The neighbors say they're little guys. Do they have, you know, weird eyes or anything?"

"Weird eyes?"

"Yeah, anything about them that's weird, if you could tell me."

I shrugged. "Why don't you ask the neighbors?"

"I will. Okay, yeah . . ."

Man, this guy was either writing the Great American Novel as we spoke or I'd said something worthy of front page headlines. I couldn't figure this dude out.

He asked me some more dumb questions and wrote several sequels while I sat on the lawn and chewed the end of a tall piece of grass. Nathan's lackadaisical about mowing the lawn, and so am I, by the way.

"Okay, great!" Chambers said, slipping his notepad into his pocket. "Listen, David . . . ?"

"Drew."

"Drew. Look, thanks for talking to me. I got some very valuable information."

"Right. I bet."

"No, really. It was a good story."

What story? I'd told him nothing but what he wanted to hear.

Nathan's beat-up old van pulled into the driveway and Nathan got out. He walked over and said hello to Chambers.

Chambers told him who he was and what he was after.

Nathan laughed. "Boy, you tabloid guys are something."

Chambers kind of laughed. "So you don't know anything about any aliens."

"Listen." Nathan got serious. "Historically, this country has been a refuge for distressed people all over the world, and I don't think there's any reason to change that now. Just because—"

"Yeah," Chambers said, looking off. "Yeah, I understand. No, really."

"I mean, just because they're not citizens is no reason to regard them as having absolutely no—"

"Right, that's true. No, I agree with you," Chambers said. "In fact, I've been active in this sort of thing myself, back when the . . . you know, a couple of years ago, when the—"

"Really? I worked for the Committee for Central American blah blah—"

They started talking about stuff I wasn't interested in, so I went back into the house.

In a little while Nathan came in and asked me what I'd told the guy. I said I'd told him absolutely nothing.

My question for Nathan, which I didn't ask, was: What do you know? We never talked about the little guys, at least not about what they really were. Nathan *had* to know that our house guests weren't Mexicans, but did he know they were aliens? Specifically, space-type aliens?

I looked at Nathan. You know, he'd not a bad-looking guy, as far as guys go. Granted, he's a little too bald to have such long hair, and sometimes he wears a pony tail in the back; not the long girl kind but the short boy kind. Taking everything into consideration, though, he doesn't look particularly weird. But sometimes he acts it. He goes into long moody periods when he doesn't talk much. And he dresses sloppily sometimes, like now: jeans with holes in them, T-shirt with a coffee stain, sandals. Not that I'm any kind of snappy dresser, you understand. I just remember this time when we went to Mom's first cousin's wedding (second marriage—or third?—I forget) and Nathan wore jeans and an old suit jacket with a snap-on tie, and sandals with white socks. I mean, Jesus Christ, Nathan.

"You understand what I said to him about Zorg and Flez?"

I was on the last page of my book. "Yeah, sure, Nathan."

"They have rights."

"I know."

"Good."

Nathan went off to the kitchen. It was his turn to cook dinner. I recently started cooking dinners. Cooking's easy if you learn a few simple fundamentals. Let me amend that. Most cooking is easy. Some things are hard to cook, I'll readily admit.

I finished *Scaramouche* and went to a book I'd been wanting to read: *Crime and Punishment*.

Chapter 9

I haven't written in a few weeks. I see I haven't dealt with the tabloid story yet, but I'll get to that in a minute.

I guess it's apparent that the intelligence drugs—or whatever they are—are having their effect. School is a snap. I'm reading much better now . . . well, that's an understatement. I zipped through Hugo's *Les Miserables* last night, in translation, unabridged version. I didn't think my French was good enough yet to tackle the original. I read Camus' *L'Etranger* in French but its style is fairly simple. Hugo, on the other hand, was a wordy old scribbler.

I've covered most of the standard American twentieth century writers: Hemingway, Faulkner, Fitzgerald, and the lot. Hemingway is a great short story writer, but a middling novelist. Fitzgerald wrote one good one, *Gatsby*. Faulkner is a genius. Now I'm reading the guys who are still around, Mailer, Styron, etc. There's so much to read. I don't think I'm going to get it all read. I have one smart pill left, and I've been debating whether to take it. That will be it for the smart pills. Will I get dumb again, regress, if I take no more? Or will I stay smart? If not, I'm worried that Zorg won't give me more. I've asked him flat out, but got a noncom-

mittal reply. Those little guys are cagey. They speak the
language fluently but everything they say is so oblique,
off-center. They dance around the subject. I think they
regret giving me the stuff. Maybe they don't want any smart
Earthlings. (There's an old sci-fi chestnut: "Earthlings." I
can't remember offhand whether Zorg or Flez have a term
that refers to Earth's inhabitants in the aggregate, except for
"your people.")

I'm getting tired of flarning. You lose sleep, and after a
few flarns, you get the general idea, and it gets boring. I do
like flying around, though. My God, I've seen . . .
what?—Antarctica, the summit of Everest, the caldera of
Kilauea, the deepest heart of the New Guinea rain forest,
and other remote sights, many of these in a single night.
(*Rain forest,* my foot. Whatever happened to *jungle*? It has
more punch. Tarzan of the Rain Forest? Rain forest fever?
Are husbands supposed to come home exhausted after a
day's work and wail, "Honey, it's a rain forest out there!")

Sure, flarning is fun. But I have an education to get, and
I still need my sleep, more so, since I've been doing all this
reading. It taxes the brain, it does.

The tabloid story broke about a week into school. Chambers
(probably a stringer) was a fast writer, and it made a great
"silly season" feature. Of course, it's always silly season at
the *World Gazette.*

The teaser headline read:

OHIO FAMILY LIVING WITH SPACE ALIENS!!!

Three exclamations points.

It was the lead story, though you were hard-pressed to
find the article, buried as it was among the diets and
horoscopes and movie star gossip. The "photograph" on the
front was very interesting. A typical American family, mom
and dad and two kids, boy and girl, she about 14, boy maybe
10, sitting around a picnic table loaded with potato salad,
corn on the cob, and fried chicken; and there, between Mom

and the boy, sat two critters with big almond-shaped cat's-eyes, melon heads, tiny bodies, and a dot for a mouth, each holding an ear of corn with spidery fingers. One big happy extended family.

At least they got the number of aliens right.

Needless to say, the family wasn't us. They didn't use our names either. This was the "Atwater family." George and Betty Atwater, and their brats, Chrissy and Tommie. This is "family values" to the max, dudes and dudesses.

I don't want to mess up these pages by transcribing the codswallop of the actual text, so this abstract will have to suffice: George and Betty, two typical Ohioans, had been receiving psychic messages from the stars, via dreams, for years, mostly from a pair of alien entities, Vlaston and Numagon. (Note the endings. Two Greek guys who are aliens, right?) Recently, the aliens, sort of interstellar ham radio operators, suggested an actual physical meeting. Well, hell, why not? George and Betty said enthusiastically, and it was more than all right with the kids, so a landing site was picked, the aliens touched down, got out of the saucer, and went home with their Earthly hosts. The saucer went back to the "mother ship." (There's always a mother ship in these stories; do I detect Freudian overtones?)

George and Betty and Vlas and Numy and the kids are having a wonderful visit together. They have been, as we can readily see, picnicking, and they have also gone boating, camping, and swimming. The family has driven them all over the place to see the sights: the local mall, McDonald's (Vlas and Numy *love* Chicken McNuggets), various community gatherings (V. & N. were the hit of the July 4th celebration). The aliens and the Atwaters (I can see the TV sit-com now) have had many long conversations, many sharings of cultural information, and the Atwaters are planning to take the spacefaring duo to DisneyWorld, all in an effort to promote greater interplanetary understanding and communication. And guess what. The aliens have invited the Atwaters to come to their home planet! Whoopee.

Oh, well, there's nothing you can do about this sort of stuff. As long as people will plunk down fifty cents for a cheap read, there will be people willing to supply the product.

The most amazing thing about that article and its repercussions, besides the fact that there are human beings with minds that can produce this kind of crapola, was that the entire neighborhood—heck, all of Keynesville—assumed that the story was about us. My assumption is that everyone in the town and its environs reads the *Gazette* with an almost religious zeal, which is a revelation in itself.

"Hey, Drew, how are the aliens?"

"Drew, dude! They take you up in that saucer yet?"

"What planet are they from? Mars or the Moon?"

And so forth. This is what echoes through the ceramic tile hallways at school.

Teachers look at me funny. I see bemusement, distrust, and maybe fear in their eyes.

The principal, Mrs. Wallace, called me to the office and asked me some very strange and roundabout questions about my "home situation." I told her everything at home was fine. She was aware that mine was a "non-traditional" family, meaning that Mom has a POSSLQ, a "person of the opposite sex sharing living quarters," that person being Nathan. She asked me how I had "internalized" that. I said I felt internally fine about it. She wanted to know if there had been any negative reactions from the "community." Regarding what? About Nathan living with us. I said no.

She asked a few more questions, most of them snoopy, and after I hemmed and hawed some more, she dismissed me.

I was late for my sexual harassment sensitivity seminar. I hear they've started them for Tyler's grade level. Can't begin too early with this stuff. All that sexual harassment

going on out in the playground, boys looking up girls'
dresses on the rain-forest gym . . .

The talk show flap started with a call for Mom, who wasn't
home. (She seldom is—when the first call from New York
came she was at her Healing Aerobics workout session,
which is, I think, some kind of holistic interpretation of
exercise. Actually, it could be warmed-over Orgone
Therapy [I read about Wilhelm Reich in Adler's biography]
for all I know.) Nathan took the call, of course, so it was he
who negotiated our appearance on the Deveaux Marsten
Show, the host of which needs no introduction if you own a
TV set and rot your brain watching controversy-mongering
talk shows.

I suppose it was the tabloid article that prompted the
show's research staff to look into the possibility of our being
guests on the show. But how they knew the article was
based on us is anybody's guess. Maybe they hired a psychic.
Seriously, they probably called Chambers and he might
have told them. However, as I said before, the fact that we
had aliens living with us seemed common knowledge.

We had become a living urban legend.

You have to keep in mind that we had had zip, zero, zilch
in the way of visits or communication from: the township
police; the state police; any federal law enforcement
agency; any state or federal investigative body, legislative
committee or such like; and we were completely ignored by
the US Immigration people, to say nothing of the Air Force,
Army, CIA, National Security Council, etc. No one even
phoned. Not even a routine computer-generated letter
floated in with the mail. But everyone in the world seemed
to take for granted that the story was true. Or at least they
were willing to take our word for it. Or at least they weren't
ready to call us liars.

You can get ahead in this world by making wild state-
ments and then leaving it up to folks to disprove you. They
usually don't, and it usually works.

Of course, tabloids print wild stories all the time, and talk show producers don't call up and ask for details. What was the difference in our case? I don't quite know, but here's my guess: the fact that there was some reality behind the myth may have given it little extra punch.

We talked it over at dinner.

"I don't believe it," Mom said. "Zorg and Flez?"

"Yeah," Nathan said. "Aliens from another world. Pretty silly, isn't it?"

I sat there eating my macaroni and cheese with broccoli. No meat this meal. That didn't worry me. What worried me was why Nathan didn't know that Zorg and Flez *were* aliens from another world.

"They could be, for all I know," Lori said as she picked at her food. She doesn't eat a lot. Except what boys buy her.

"Don't be silly," Mom said. "They don't look like aliens."

"What do aliens look like?" I demanded.

"I really couldn't say," Mom said. "But they can't look like Zorg and Flez."

"I don't know, take away their Hawaiian shirts and gabardine slacks and what do you have?"

"Two funny-looking little guys in their underwear," Lori said, then laughed.

Tyler giggled and nearly snarfed his milk.

"Right, I said. They look funny. If you look at them real hard, they don't even look human. They look humanoid."

"What does that mean, exactly?" Mom asked me.

"It means like unto a human. Humanlike but not exactly."

"Have you been reading the dictionary lately?" Nathan said with a smile.

"Yeah, I guess I have been."

"He does nothing but read," Mom said to Nathan. "It's really amazing. He never did that before. I mean, I think it's wonderful . . ."

"I think you'll notice the improvement at report card time," I said.

"Anyway, this talk show thing," Mom went on. "Nathan, they want us all to be on the show?"

"Yeah. I think it would be fun."

"But why, Nathan? What do they want with us?"

"The producer I talked to was pretty vague about it. At this point I think the topic is going to be something like urban myths."

"Urban myths? We live in the country."

"Just a term. He brought up a number of possible angles. The modern non-traditional American family . . . oh, we talked about a lot of things. I suggested a debate about the illegal alien issue."

"What's non-traditional about us?" Mom wanted to know. "Man, woman, kids. We're a family, period."

"Well, we aren't *exactly* legal," Nathan said slyly. "According to traditional mores—"

"We're common law. I keep telling you, Nathan, we're common law spouses."

Nathan conceded the point. "We've been together long enough."

"You better believe it. So, like I always say, why not sign a marriage certificate and make it all official-legal?"

"We will, Cheryl, we will."

She appealed to me. "It's up to you to see that this man makes an honest woman of me."

"I'm old enough to own a shotgun in this state," I told Nathan.

He grinned. "You're not old enough to buy one yourself. I'd have to sign for it."

"You mean I would," Mom said. "And I'll do it."

Nathan chuckled.

"So," I said. "Are we going to do it? The talk show."

Mom shrugged. "I don't know if I can get off work. And what about school?"

"Won't hurt 'em to miss a day," Nathan said. "And maybe we could make it over a school holiday. They'll fly us to New York, you know."

"Oh, that's nice," Mom said.

"It is true that they didn't care much for the non-traditional angle," Nathan confessed. "They thought maybe I was talking about two gay men raising kids. But when I told them you were—"

"But it's the alien thing they're interested in," I said. "Not us as a non-whatever family."

"Yeah. But it's so stupid."

"I don't know about that," I said. "Lots of people are interested in flying saucers."

"That's true," Mom agreed. "Everybody at work watches Star Trek."

I chewed my mouthful with a frown. "Uh, what's that got to do with flying saucers?"

"Oh, you know, outer space and all that stuff."

"Oh."

"I forgot to add that they'd pay us for being on the show," Nathan said.

"Great!" Lori said.

"Great!" Tyler echoed.

"I didn't know that," Mom said, genuinely amazed. "I thought all those people went on for free."

"Have you ever watched Deveaux?"

"Hmm? Oh, a couple of times. But he's on in the day, isn't he?"

"Yeah," Nathan said. "He's one of the more articulate hosts. He's African-American, did you know that?"

"Oh. No, I didn't. Funny, I don't remember him being that."

"Uh, well, he really doesn't look it much. I think he's only part black."

"Anyway," I said. "Are we going or not?"

"Let me think about it," Mom said.

If you're thinking that Mom made most of the big decisions around the house, you're right. After all, it was her house. I don't think Nathan ever had a house. He was married before, that I know; but he must be numbered among the houseless.

You know, now that I think of it, my general knowledge of Nathan's past life is on the skimpy side. Funny I didn't realize it before. But no matter.

No official visits or investigations, but oh boy, did we get unofficial snoopers. And I'm not talking about tabloid reporters or general media people.

UFO "investigators," so-called.

It began with a phone call from a guy who was with some kind of local UFO network. His name was Wayne Milburn.

"I'm vice-president of the county chapter of the Ohio Skywatch Network. We're a UFO tracking and investigation outfit. All volunteer, of course."

"Yeah," I said cautiously. "What do you want?"

"Well, we've had an incredible number of reports from your area. It's been one of the biggest sources of UFO sightings we've ever had around here. And your particular location seems to be the source of it all."

"Uh-huh. So?"

"Uh . . . well, we'd like to interview you. And if you don't mind, we'd like to come over there and take some readings."

This guy sounded young. I couldn't place the age, but he couldn't have been much over twenty-five. The voice was high-pitched but not effeminate—just young. Yet I knew he wasn't a kid. Maybe he never grew up?

Okay, the problem was keeping him away from the house. I ruminated a moment on the best tactic to take.

"You can interview me," I said.

"Huh? Oh, yeah. Sure. But . . . well, it's your parents I'd like to talk to mostly. Not that I don't want to interview the kids, but—"

"It's me you want to talk to," I said. "I'm the one who knows more about the aliens."

"Oh, yeah? Wow. All right. Hey, you mean you really have seen aliens?"

"Sure."

"Great."

The ensuing pause gave me to understand that he was scribbling.

"Yeah, right. Now, when did you first see these aliens? First, what do they look like? Big eyes, little bodies, about four feet tall? We get a lot of those."

I could hear Nathan coming downstairs.

"Listen, you'll have to call back," I said hurriedly. "I'll call you back. What's your number?"

"What's the problem? If I could talk to your—"

"Where are you?"

"Huh?"

"I'll come and see you."

"Well, I'm in Keynesville, but—"

"No problem, I'll come."

"Well, okay . . ."

He gave me his address, and a few directions. By that time Nathan had walked through the living room and gone down to the basement without bothering to inquire who was on the phone.

"Really, I could come out there and interview the whole—"

"No, it's better this way. I'll be there in about . . . oh, about an hour."

Chapter 10

Wayne Milburn was the first saucer "expert" to call, but he wasn't the last. I may get around to describing some of the others in detail eventually, but I have to say that my general impression of these people isn't favorable. In fact, I'd be willing to venture that most of them are several bricks shy of a load. There may be some serious researchers among all the flakes, but by and large your typical UFO investigator, "scientifically trained, technically sophisticated, serious in intent and purpose" . . . or so reads the Ohio Skywatch Network charter (I have it here) . . . is an eccentric in the grand tradition; or, to put it less kindly, a raving nut case with a less than robust sense of reality. I don't *think* I'm being unfair. I've been reading about these guys.

These guys will believe anything you tell them. (There are few women in this field, I noted.) When they go out in the field they bring all their fancy paraphernalia: Geiger counters, magnetometers, oscilloscopes, photon multipliers, radio direction finders, etc., etc., and it all sounds pretty impressive. But it's mostly show. Sure, they know how to calibrate their instruments and use them, and they gather all sorts of data that show up as numbers on screens and squiggles on paper and blotches on still more screens; data which, I suppose, they take home and process the living bejesus out of.

Technical sophistication they have in abundance. What they don't have a lot of is plain old common sense.

Rather than sketch the general contours of this mentality, however, I'll simply direct your attention to the strange case of Wayne Milburn.

It didn't take an hour to get into Keynesville by bike, but I wanted some leeway. I wanted to check this guy out first, look over where he lived, case the joint. You can never tell about people these days. Bizarre behavior seems more commonplace than ever, and old Wayne did not come highly recommended in the normality department. I had deduced that right off the bat.

Keynesville is a small old farming town that a bunch of suburbs and shopping malls have sprung up around like mushrooms. There are lots of recent housing developments surrounding the old sections, and Wayne lived in one of these latter.

The street was typically Small Town, right out of Sherwood Anderson or Sinclair Lewis, lined with oak and beech and a few horse chestnut trees. The turn-of-the-century houses were mostly two or two and a half stories with clapboard siding painted white or blue-gray, stately and prim, prosperous but not ostentatious. Middle class to the core. I pedaled up to the address, stood my bike up on its kickstand, and looked the place over.

This one had gone a little to seed, needed a paint job. A hanging jungle of sucker vines had colonized the entire north side of the house. The forsythia along the front side sprouted wildly, and the lawn needed mowing. There were stacks of boxes and piles of odd junk on the porch, and from the look of the weathering I guessed the stuff had been there a while.

For all that, however, the place didn't look spooky, didn't

fit the part of the lair of some ax murderer. Satisfied that my life wasn't in danger, I went to the front door and pressed the doorbell button. Nothing happened, so I knocked.

A while passed before the door was opened by a middle-aged woman in a flower print dress and a checked apron. She had gray hair and wrinkles around her gray eyes; I put her age at around fifty-five. She smiled pleasantly and asked who I was, and I told her I was supposed to see Wayne.

"He's where he usually is, down in his haunt in the cellar. Sometimes I think he lives there. You can go around back or come through the house."

"I'll go around back."

After a trip through high grass and wild weeds, negotiating en route with a gate that didn't want to open, I arrived at the cellar entrance, a back door to what looked like an addition. I knocked.

I heard a voice yell, but couldn't make it out. I knocked again and this time I clearly heard, "Come on in, it's not locked—and watch your step!"

I went in.

The door immediately gave onto steep wooden steps that went down to a cluttered but semifinished basement: fake wood paneling and plywood covered the walls, and fluorescent light fixtures illuminated the place fairly well. A door in the far wall led off to other, darker sections of the cellar.

The back and side walls were covered with elaborate tiers of metal shelving, and on this framework sat every conceivable communications device known to man. There was a wide assortment of CB radios, police scanners, shortwave sets, walkie-talkies, cellular phones, conventional phones, computers, and what looked like an intercom or two, along with amplifiers, tuners, and other auxiliary gear.

I approached this display of electronic clutter. A man was seated at a desk nestled in a U-shaped declivity among the racks, his back to me, talking into one of about a dozen microphones.

I didn't get the drift of the conversation, distracted as I was by everything around me. The racks weren't the only item of interest. Competing for attention was the rest of the place and the interesting junk in it. Against the walls stood rows of doorless old refrigerators holding many a quaint and curious item, most of which would be hard to describe. Oddments, doodads, thingamajigs—old electric motors, maybe, half-disassembled. I walked around and looked at everything while he continued talking.

Finally the conversation wound up, and the guy—Wayne Milburn, I presumed—pushed the desk microphone away.

He turned and looked at me. He wasn't as young as I figured but he was still in his twenties, maybe early thirties. He had a bush of thick black hair and a heavy beard shadow, and wore thick glasses. His face was full, chin a bit weak, and he sported a crimson pimple or two, though his face wasn't teen-pimply.

His expression was strange. He looked as though he had a grave and momentous announcement to make; but underneath was a smirk.

"Things are approaching a panic situation," he intoned. He gave it sort of a dramatic reading.

This produced in me an equally strange effect. A fireworks burst of possibilities flashed through my mind. Something was happening, some disaster had just happened and he had learned about it over the CB radio—

Well, my secret was out. The police had shown up at the house just after I left and taken Zorg and Flez away.

Blog had landed on the White House lawn and demanded that Earth give up Zorg and Flez.

No, I hadn't forgotten about Blog, and was in fact still pondering, in the back of my mind, the question of who or what Blog could be. Moreover, as the smart pills gave me the ability to gain perspective on things, I started to worry.

But now things were *approaching a panic situation.* Great, wonderful.

"What is it?" I said breathlessly.

"Bigfoot."

"I—" I probably did a classic comic take. "Huh?"

"Haven't you been hearing about all the sightings? We're in the middle of one of the biggest Bigfoot flaps ever."

I exhaled a cloud of relief. "Oh," I said.

"It's been hectic here, let me tell you," Milburn went on. "Calls have been pouring in from all over the Midwest. It's been sighted in fourteen counties in Ohio alone."

"What's been sighted?"

"Didn't I say? Bigfoot."

"Oh. You're a Bigfoot expert, then, not flying saucers?"

He poked a finger in my direction. "We've proved that Bigfoot and UFOs are related. *Proved* it. I have hard evidence . . . *incontrovertible* evidence that links them."

"No kidding. Bigfoots . . . er, Bigfeet are space aliens?"

"We don't really know," Milburn told me. "They may be biots."

"Yeah? What're those?"

"Biological robots, artificial creatures. Androids."

"What are they supposed to do?"

"We're not quite sure," Milburn said with a frown. "It's a mystery. Remember the movie *The Day the Earth Stood Still*?"

"Uh-huh, I think."

"Remember Gort, the robot? *Klatuu barada nicto*, and all that? The Bigfoots and the saucer occupants may have some kind of symbiotic relationship. The Bigfoots might even be in control."

"No kidding. That's really something." I nodded, profoundly impressed by these startling revelations.

"You bet. That's what we do in Oz Net."

"In what?"

"Ohio Skywatch Network. We call it OSNet for short. You know, Oz, Wizard of Oz?"

"Right. What exactly do you do in OSNet?"

"We gather data and come up with theories, hypotheses, and then we go into the field after more data that either proves or disproves the hypotheses. It's very scientific. We're not a bunch of saucer cultists going around making wild claims. We have science and technology backing us up. We're not saucer nuts." Milburn gravely shook his head.

"You're not saucer nuts." I just as gravely shook my head.

"No. The field is rife with loonies. Crazy people who don't know reality from their fantasies. And hoaxers. We've exposed any number of out-and-out bamboozlers. Con artists."

I was wondering if I'd buy a used saucer from Wayne Milburn. Yeah, I guess I would, I thought. There was something sincere about him.

"Say, how old are you?" Milburn wanted to know.

"Thirteen. Why, am I too young?"

Milburn laughed. "Oh, no, sometimes kids make the best witnesses. They haven't learned to hold back for fear of ridicule. That's what keeps most people from reporting strange phenomena, you know. Fear, plain fear of the neighbors laughing."

My neighbors didn't laugh, I thought. They finked on us.

"So, what can I do for you?" Milburn said.

"Well, I thought you wanted to interview me."

"Yeah, right. You're . . . ?"

"Drew Hayes."

"Hayes, right, right. Didn't think you'd show, really. Thought you were just blowing me off on the phone, there."

"No," I said. "I thought I should talk to somebody about this, someone who knows more than I do about these things."

It was true that this was in the back of my mind. Seeing Milburn in his kooky element now, though, I was entertaining doubts.

"You should talk with somebody."

Milburn swiveled around and flipped a switch or two, then got up and fetched from the metal shelves a handful of gear. It was, he said, a wireless microphone, radio-linked to a tape recorder that was now running. He pinned the tiny mike on my shirt collar and hung the other gadget, the transmitter, from the belt of my jeans.

"There, that should do it. Just speak naturally. Here, have a seat."

He extricated a battered wooden chair from some debris.

I sat. "Okay, what do you want me to say?"

Milburn reseated himself at his master console. "Well, whatever you want. Now . . . uh . . . let's see, you're a contactee, right?"

"I'm the— We're the family that has aliens living with us."

"Right, I knew that, but I just want to state things for the record. This is a document, you understand. Okay, we're still rolling. Now . . ."

"What are you going to do with the tape?" I demanded.

"Huh? It'll go into the archives, after it's been analyzed and . . . you know, collated, and stuff. Okay, I want to ask you some questions. First, give your full name and address."

I did.

"Okay," Milburn said, "When and where did you first see the aliens, who, you say, are now living with you? By the way, you live with your family, right? Mother and dad? Sisters, brothers?"

I told him all that, leaving out the part about Nathan and Mom not being married.

"Good, good," Milburn said. "Great. Now, in your own words and to the best of your ability, describe what took place the first time that you had these Close Encounters."

Milburn gave me an expectant look. The smirk was just part of his basic facial expression, I decided.

My, those glasses were thick. The guy was as blind as a bat. How many UFO's could he have seen personally? Not many, was my conjecture.

"Uh . . . okay." I took a deep breath, and began.

I spilled the beans, basically, told him everything, holding nothing back. Maybe I embellished a little in spots, and it

could be that I nipped and tucked in other places, for
brevity's sake; but essentially I gave him the whole story.

He absorbed it all enthusiastically, jotting down a few
notes on a legal pad affixed to a clipboard.

"Great, great. This is really nice stuff. Now, have Zork
and Phlegm ever said—"

"Zorg and Flez."

"Yeah. They've never said where they're from? What
planet?"

"No, though I gather it's a long way off. Light-years."

"Right. You know a little about astronomy, then?"

I nodded. "Sure, a little."

"Yeah, they could be from another galaxy entirely,"
Milburn said. "Who knows? Great."

Next he asked me questions about weather conditions at
the time of the sighting and if any power lines were near. I
made up answers. In the middle of an interstellar visitation,
who the heck would notice how humid it was or have a clue
as to the barometric pressure? And who would care?

Power lines. Sure, there might have been some nearby.
But it was dark, Wayne. Dark. Like, no light? These were
silly questions.

"Okay," Milburn said. "Now, you say that these aliens,
the ones you picked up on the road, are still living with you,
and have been for the past . . . how long has it been?"

"Since July."

"Since July. Okay, it's nearly October. And they periodi-
cally go out in their flying saucer . . . uh, which they
keep . . ." He kept scribbling.

"In a duffel bag," I finished for him.

"In a . . . duffel . . ."

Boy, this guy liked to scribble, too, but he was slower
than the reporter.

"Bag," I helped. It sounded even more ridiculous when
you said it slowly.

"Bag . . . Yeah. Okay, well, that's something new.

Never had a report quite like this before. You know, collapsible saucer, and all. That's pretty unique."

"There can be only one degree of uniqueness," I informed him.

"Yeah." He was looking at his notes and nodding.

I think he was losing interest.

"Were there any markings on the craft? You know, signs, symbols?"

"Nope."

"And the color was . . . did you say?"

"Greenish gray."

"Greenish gray. Uh-huh. No markings of any kind?"

"No markings."

"None?"

"None."

He seemed a bit disappointed by this. "Well, that seems to be everything. This is a fairly unusual report. We've had all kinds over the years—aliens coming to visit, staying for tea or something, but never any . . . you know, live-in aliens."

"Boarding aliens," I offered.

"Yeah, no boarding aliens. Are they . . . I mean, are they paying you anything for this?"

"No."

"And you're feeding them?"

"No. I guess it should be 'rooming aliens,' because they don't eat our food."

"They brought their own food?"

"I've never seen them eat, really," I confessed. It was true. "I don't know exactly how they survive. Their ship, though, can do anything. I'd bet that it synthesizes food for them."

"Right!" Milburn said, methodically scrawling again. He liked that. "Great."

Right then I noticed something, a sign above the racks, big as life, announcing that this was BIGFOOT CONTROL.

Bigfoot Control.

I sighed.

"Another unusual thing," Milburn said, "is the way your aliens look. We don't get many completely human-looking aliens these days. Used to, back in the nineteen-fifties. But recently UFO occupants have tended to be sort of weird-looking."

"Tell me something," I said. "How did you find out about us?"

"OSNet. Reports have been coming in all summer about some alien presence in the area. There have been any number of sightings of your aliens' saucer. And then came the rumors about aliens living with a family. But accounts conflicted about which family it was. There was this one family up in . . . I forget where the heck they were. Anyway, I'm glad we had this interview, because when the talk show people called up—"

"Talk show people?"

"Yeah. I forget the guy's name . . . I never watch TV much."

"Deveaux Marsten?"

"Yeah, that one. They're going to do a show about UFO's in this area and they wanted me to be in on it. I said sure, and they said they'd call back. But they haven't yet."

"We're supposed to be on that show. My family."

"No kidding?" Milburn said.

I was puzzled. "You mean you didn't know? Then how did you know we were the family with the aliens?"

"Some woman who lives across from you called up and said you were the ones, so I looked up your number in the phone book."

Mrs. Carey strikes a blow for Earth vs. the flying saucers. Small world.

"I haven't seen any Bigfeet, by the way," I said.

"What? Oh, yeah. You haven't? Well, not all saucer sightings have a Bigfoot connection. I never said that, I just meant that—"

"What *is* all this stuff down here?" I said, suddenly rising.

"Oh, I like to tinker," Wayne said.

A genuine basement crank inventor. Actually, I kind of liked the big guy. He was kooky, but friendly and completely harmless. And his naive enthusiasm was kind of . . . well, charming in a way.

He showed me various projects. In a far corner of the basement he was reassembling a Model T engine.

"Hard to get parts," he said. "If you buy them from the specialty parts dealers, the ones that deal in antique stuff, you pay through the nose. I like to go out to junk yards and search."

"Junk yards still have car parts from the nineteen-twenties?"

"Oh, those Model T's lasted well into the fifties in some places."

"Uh-huh. What's this?"

"That's a letterpress printer. I publish a couple of newsletters. Hand-set type."

There was other print hardware: several mimeograph machines, an outmoded wet-copy copier (inoperative), and an ancient hectograph.

It went on and on, this catalog from a white elephant sale, this endless flea market. The place was full of interesting, quirky stuff.

Then there was the depository of UFO "evidence." Also Bigfoot "specimens."

Specimens?

"Hair samples, mostly," Milburn said, sifting through a bin holding plastic bags full of fuzz. "And stool."

"Stool."

"Dung. Shit."

"You have a collection of Bigfoot shit?"

"Yeah, probably the most extensive collection in the East. Here's the most recent sample. Comes from a farm near Cincinnati."

He brought out a pail with some dark matter in it.

I bent and peered down. It looked like shit, all right.

I had no further questions for Mr. Wayne Milburn, and he had none for me.

After delivering me from the radio mike rig, he thanked me for the interview. I said, hey, no problem.

As I was going up the steps he called out, "You know, you're pretty intelligent for your age."

"Thanks."

"By the way, you should come to one of our meetings. OSNet, I mean. We meet every Thursday night at St. Pamphylia's church hall."

"St. Pamphylia. Right. Well, so long."

"See you, Drew. Come back anytime."

"Thanks. Bye."

I left.

Chapter 11

I should mention the abductions, or at least what abductions there were before I put a stop to them.

The "sport" of randomly nabbing people is part and parcel, I discovered, of the art of flarning. Zorg and Flez didn't look upon it as anything essentially harmful. I went along at first, thinking myself merely an observer; but when it became clear that further acquiescence could be interpreted as complicity, I put my foot down. To my surprise, Zorg and Flez valued my opinion, and honored my request.

Looking back, I suppose we flarned more times that summer than I've let on, but the omission isn't due to intentional dishonesty. No doubt I've done some repressing. (Or Kel, the ship, engineered my repression, before my increased intelligence allowed me to overcome Kel's machinations—but I digress. I'll get to that later.)

If memory serves (though it doesn't necessarily, as I mentioned), the first abductees were a teenage couple who were unlucky enough to be copulating on the grass of a public park when our ship swooped over them in the darkness. As near as I can pinpoint the location, this was somewhere near, or perhaps in, Mobile, Alabama.

The word for abduction, by the way, in Zorg and Flez's "language" (I wish I could go into the reason for the quotes, but there simply isn't room here, and I'm not sure I understand it myself completely. Would you take my word for it that the quotes are appropriate? Thanks.) is *vlom*. Right, you've noticed the tendency toward monosyllabism.

The floor dilated and up they came, she completely naked, he with his jeans around his ankles. This was an education for me, as you no doubt would guess. I had never seen people in the act before, except for soft-core approximations in slick magazines. But here was the real thing, two people caught in flagrante delicto, as it were. The boy's erection was impressive; however, it quickly wilted.

The bodies came up and floated, turning slowly like chickens on a rotisserie. I watched, fascinated. Neither of the abductees uttered a sound. The girl's face was frozen in a silent scream, the boy's in an expression of puzzlement mixed with fear.

I think they were conscious, or semiconscious. As I said, I was fascinated—at first. Then when I realized that I could be considered an accessory to a felonious act, I got scared.

What was the reaction of our galactic friends, the DeVito brothers? They were laughing themselves silly, sounding like two canaries who'd gobbled peyote buttons.

But I didn't say anything, that first time. Nor the second, either. The nabbee that time was an elderly man in a panama hat and tropical suit, out for an evening constitutional. He couldn't have been less than ninety years old. I was afraid he'd die on the spot, and was about to say something, when Zorg and Flez suddenly lost interest in him and let him go.

But the third time . . .

That was the jogger, a young woman. They stripped her of her Nike jogging suit—it was slick, you'd just have to see how it was done to appreciate it—and rotated her a bit. And then things appeared out of nowhere, out of the walls, I suppose: instruments, probes, and other weirdly wicked gadgets. At first I had no idea what they were, but didn't like the look of them.

Then the ghastly realization came: they were going to give her a medical examination. All very proper, I'm sure, strictly in the interest of advancing the cause of alien science.

"Hey!" I yelled. "You can't do that!"

Kel promptly dressed the woman and lowered her through the dilated hatch to the ground.

I told Zorg that we shouldn't do that any more.

"Why not? It's fun."

"Yeah, but it's wrong."

"Wrong?"

I thought he was having trouble grasping the concept, because he looked vaguely puzzled; but apparently Zorg was very well acquainted with the concept of moral wrong-doing, because he said, "Sure, but . . . you know, it's fun."

"Uh-huh, sometimes—but it's still wrong. Besides, it's . . . *weird.*"

"Awww . . ."

So we vlommed no more.

I guess I should tell you about the talk show.

It was a disaster.

First of all, we didn't even get to New York. The TV studio where the Deveaux Marsten Show taped was in New Jersey, out in the middle of a marsh somewhere. The hotel, properly a motel, was nearby, a highway-hugging Sheraton. The production people told us that the company had just made the move. Manhattan was getting just too expensive, and what with the economy on the fritz, etc.

New York wasn't far away, but we never got there. No time. We had one night at the Sheraton, only one, and our plane tickets had us on an early flight back to Columbus the next day. The show was taped at six o'clock, and we had no sooner checked into the Sheraton when the limo arrived to cart us to the studio. Taping took the better part of three hours, though the show's air time ran only one. So, we'd be free at 9 PM—but that's a tad late to drive into Manhattan and do anything consequential, except to take in a night spot or two, which we couldn't with underage kiddies.

Right, no New York. I would have been disappointed had I not, just two nights previous, hovered over the tops of the World Trade Center, the Chrysler Building, and the Empire State, taking in the sights. (Would you believe that this brazen act elicited not one police call in any of the five boroughs of New York? Not one. Apparently nobody spotted the ship, or if so, did not regard it as anything unusual.)

I had never been in a television studio before. The place looked for the most part like an industrial building, concrete and steel and few windows. Inside, it was like a cave. What seemed like a thousand lighting fixtures hung from an elaborate metal grid above. The spacious floor was of an indeterminate gray linoleum, very smooth, and mostly flat, except for the perimeter, which curved up toward the walls, producing some sort of distance effect on camera, no doubt. Otherwise, the floor was as wide and as flat as a football field, with a half-dozen large studio cameras, manned by cameramen (and one camerawoman), gliding about it.

The seats for the audience were done up in high bleachers. The layout wasn't like a theater, where you come in on one level and the seats slope down to the stage or screen. You had to mount stairs to the seats.

Other than that, the place was fairly nondescript.

On arrival, we were ushered into the Green Room. And who should we find sitting there, looking uncomfortable in a discount department store suit and badly tied, garish four-in-hand, sucking a can of diet ginger ale? None other than Wayne Milburn. There was another guy there I recognized: the science fiction writer Trafford Starnes, whom I remembered from the news tape. He was maybe fifty. Portly but just short of being fat, he wore a gray beard to distract from a genuinely homely, almost porcine face.

His long curly gray hair crawled down to the stained collar of a sort of African safari jacket that draped over a black T-shirt. The shirt bore something indecipherable on it. He didn't introduce himself but smiled crookedly at us when we came in.

I said hello to Wayne and introduced him to my family. He looked nervous, but we chatted amiably until the show's producer came in to talk to us.

He introduced himself. Hal Estermann was his name, and he wore a very finely tailored suit, though the weave of the material was a little on the flashy side for an outfit as expensive as I guessed this one to be. He was bald, looked sixtyish, maybe older, and he came in smoking a huge cocoa-colored cigar, which was remarkable in this day and age. I mean, they don't let you go around many public places puffing a cigarette, much less blowing out clouds from something that looks like a piece of dog matter. But maybe he owned the studio and could do as he pleased. Whatever, the cigar stank.

He told us he went back a long way in television, starting out as a floor manager on the original Milton Berle show (I had seen kinescopes of TV incunabula, and so knew who and what he meant) back in the late nineteen-forties. Since then, he'd worked on many a TV show in various capacities, and had done a stint in Hollywood making movies. He mentioned some titles, all of which rang no bells. After Tinseltown, it was back to New York and daytime TV.

"Soaps, game shows, I line-produced 'em all," Hal Estermann told us, thick lips moving around that stupendous smoking stalk.

He started to explain the show's format when he was interrupted by people arriving—more guests, it looked like. One of them caught my eye, a blond girl my age who looked really terrific. Mr. Estermann told us they were in the show's second segment—"Sex-changing Parents." No kidding, that was the topic. Which kind of intrigued me. I mean, you could have sex-changing fathers—dads who became female. (Did that make them moms? Sheesh, no end of variations on this theme.) But moms becoming dads?

Estermann continued to go over the show's format, how the time for each segment was equally divided between exchanges between guests and host, guests and audience, and host and audience. They liked to keep the show moving; but don't worry, dead spots would be edited out; and, by the way, bad language would be bleeped, so we were ill-advised to use it. The show ran an hour on the air, but would take longer to tape, etc.

"I'd like to ask you something, Mr. Estermann," Nathan said.

"Call me Hal. Sure, go ahead."

"What's the topic of our segment?"

"That's what I wanted to go over with you. We've been haggling over this. Deveaux doesn't go for the idea of a show about flying saucers, per se."

Wayne Milburn looked puzzled.

"Good," Nathan said. "So, what's the topic?"

"Well, it's kind of awkward, it being almost taping time, but we *think* we're going to go with 'Middle American Fantasies,' or something like that. We're going to cover all the myths—aliens, Elvis sightings . . . what else?—" Estermann beckoned for suggestions.

"Bigfoot?" Milburn said helpfully, and hopefully.

Estermann snapped his fingers at him. "Yeah! Bigfoot, good one. You're the Bigfoot expert, right?"

"Yeah, and UFO's, too, but I'm a serious researcher, not a myth-chaser. I have documentary proof of a huge government cover-up that's been ongoing for thirty years, and—"

He was cut short by a derisory guffaw issuing from Trafford Starnes.

Mr. Estermann grinned. "Right, good stuff, but we'll get to that when we tape. Good material, that's exactly what we want."

"If it's bullshit you want, you'll get it," Trafford Starnes said. "There's plenty of that around."

Estermann smiled at him. "Here's our devil's advocate We like to get opposing views, of course."

"I'm your man," Starnes asserted.

"Good, wonderful. I'm sure we're going to have a terrific show."

"What about the alternative family?" Nathan asked.

"What about it?" Estermann said.

"Are we going to get into, you know, alternative family styles, living arrangements, that sort of thing?"

"'Alternative family styles,' I like that, I like that," Estermann mused. "Yeah, well, we've done a lot of that recently. Gay couples with kids, gay kids with straight parents, and today we have more family stuff on the second segment."

"Then why did you want our whole family on the show?" Mom asked.

"Well, it is a family segment, but it's Middle American," Estermann said. "Family values, traditional stuff, like that. You know?"

Nathan began, "But we're not—"

Mom kicked him.

Estermann chose not to notice the byplay. "Okay, we're going to get rolling here in a couple of minutes. Look, I want you all not to be nervous. I want you to relax, have fun. Pretend it's just a discussion going on in your living room, like you're throwing a get-together for a couple of friends. Above all, relax. Talk naturally . . ."

He went on with his warm-up, if that's what it was. I guess on a show like this you have to warm up the guests as well as the audience. But he didn't tell any jokes. I wish he had.

Estermann went over to talk with the other guests. What I thought were two women with the blonde were in fact a woman and a man in drag. These were the girl's parents? I certainly hoped not.

Estermann left, and a makeup crew came in, a man and a woman. They went to work on Nathan and Mom first. A young production assistant, a girl, came in to take Tyler away. She'd be watching him during the show. They thought Tyler just a little young to be on the show; I don't know why. He put up a fuss, but finally left with the girl, reluctantly.

After Estermann left I had an idea. Normally I would have sat and pined after the blonde, but with increased intelligence came some boldness, as a bonus. I got up and approached the sex-indeterminate family.

"Hi, I'm Drew Hayes. Me and my family's going to be on the show, too. If you folks want something to drink, all that stuff on that table, there, is for the guests. The production people served us, but it looks like they're busy. Can I get you a drink?"

The woman, who wasn't bad-looking—in fact she was kind of pretty—smiled at me. "That's nice of you, Drew. Thank you."

The guy dressed like a woman said, "I could use a drink. Do they serve alcohol?"

His voice wasn't at all womanish.

"Uh, I don't think so. They didn't offer any to us."

"No, I guess not, family show and all."

The man got up and went to the table, which was laden with ice, glasses, and soft-drink cans. "What'll it be, honey?"

"Diet Pepsi . . . uh, Georgette."

I looked at the girl. She was smiling at me nicely. I liked that smile. A lot. Her teeth sparkled like snow-capped mountains in the early spring sun. Wow.

The thunderbolt hit.

"Can . . . can I get you a drink?" I asked daringly.

She grinned. "Thank you. Diet Coke, no caffeine, if they have it."

"Sure, I think they do."

I went and got it for her.

Her dad's perfume was suffocatingly florid.

I brought back the can, along with a plastic glass full of ice.

The girl accepted it gratefully, as if I'd done her a great boon.

"Gee, thanks. My name's Kristina Peerson."

"Nice to meet you." I sort of bowed. I don't know why.

Whatever, it didn't go over badly. Kristina's smile turned even brighter. Peerson. Swedish? Yeah. Arctic snows, pure and drifting. Reindeer grazing beneath the northern lights.

"Nice to meet you, Drew," Mrs. Peerson said. "This is my husband. His name was George but now he likes to be called Georgette. He's going to be a transsexual very soon."

"As soon as we can afford the operation," Georgette said, sitting back down with a drink.

Ye Gods, what can you say to that?

"That's nice," I said.

"Where are you from?" Kristina asked.

I was glad she was taking the lead in the conversation. Doubled IQ or none, I was still a little nervous about talking to girls.

We had a nice conversation, exchanging city and school info, that sort of basic stuff, until it was my turn for makeup. Some woman patted my face down with a moist pad, and then dusted me, padded some more, dusted again. I sneezed, and everyone laughed, including Kristina.

It was just a quick makeup job. They didn't give guests full makeup for the show, too time-consuming. Besides, they wanted people to be "natural, the way they really are." Hmm. Features washed out in harsh studio lights, natural?

Kristina was from Minneapolis. I asked if it got really cold there during the winter.

"Sure, but I've lived there all my life. I laugh it off."

I liked that. She laughed it off. Her eyes were very blue.

Needless to say, I fell instantly in love. Of course, it was safe for me to do that. Tomorrow, Kristina would be on a plane bound for Minneapolis, some 800 miles away from Keynesville, Ohio, and I wouldn't have to deal with the part about whether or not she was in love with me, which she probably wasn't. Parting is such sweet sorrow, wouldst fain . . . and all that noise. Oh, hell.

I was instantly depressed.

But. . . .

Wait a minute. I thought, what's eight hundred miles to Kel, the magic spaceship? A stone's throw. Down the street. Roll out of bed and you're there.

The notion that Zorg and Flez's wacky alien vehicle could be put to some practical use entered my lovesick brain for the first time.

Chapter 12

"Places, everyone!"

It was show time. After I said goodbye to Kristina, we filed out into the corridor that connected the Green Room to the studio. Following one of the production assistants, we went through a pair of enormous steel doors and out into the studio.

And there was the audience. They looked calm enough. I'd watched the show a couple of times, and Deveaux Marsten's audiences could get fairly exercised. Marsten is an expert at audience manipulation.

We took our places on the set. The seats were comfortable, maybe a little too comfortable. I was tired. Plane rides make me sleepy for some reason, or maybe it's travel generally that induces a sort of blah feeling: a malaise, as ze French say. I know I have to sleep more when I travel.

I looked up at the lights. Thousands of them—but in reality merely hundreds, probably, festooned with hanging cables and wires and ropes, along with other weird contraptions I couldn't readily identify.

I looked down to see the star of the show striding onto the set.

"Greetings, everybody!" he said brightly. He had a good voice.

"Hi, Mr. Marsten," I said, giving him a smile.

"Just call me Deveaux. We're going to have a great show. Just relax, Okay?"

"Sure!"

He was tall, well built and had some looks, and those looks were unusual. He had curly but not kinky hair, and a rather wide, flat nose. The dark eyes were spaced well apart. The lips were full. Yes, he did look African-American, in a way.

In a way, though, his skin was no darker than, say, the average Mediterranean's. Maybe you could say he had a Levantine look about him. Be that as it may, this guy was well removed from his black forbears. An octaroon, maybe. The French first name made that a little more likely, I thought.

All in all, though, he was a personable young man. He was still young, maybe edging up the slope toward forty. His suit was magnificent—not that it was ostentatious. The taste was impeccable, and the tailor must have charged him a bundle.

A couple more minutes passed, as last-minute preparations were made. Cameramen pushed cameras into position. Technicians scurried about, doing all sorts of things with cables and wires and whatnot. One of them came up to each of us and attached our wireless microphones. He clipped mine to the breast pocket of my shirt. They were tiny little things, much smaller than the one Wayne had used.

I was getting nervous just sitting there. Mom was beside me. She reached and squeezed my hand. I felt better. Mom can always do that, make me feel better.

Suddenly, there was music and Marsten was talking into a wireless mike that looked like an oversized flashlight. I wondered why it was so big.

"Welcome to another show, ladies and gentlemen. I'm Deveaux Marsten—and today we're dealing with American fantasies. Urban myths, modern fantasies about life and reality and the universe . . ."

I was watching the monitor. The camera framed Deveaux's handsome face in a tight close-up. He looked out at the home audience with a puzzled, almost painful frown.

"What is with Middle Americans, today? They seem to live in a cross between Disneyland and a sci-fi flick. Everyone's a space cadet. Flying saucers are back, they're all the rage now, but these days people aren't just seeing them in the skies. Flying saucers are landing in our back yards, in our driveways. Aliens are here. But they're not just landing. They're coming to dinner! They're staying over! We have a family here who claims to have aliens living with them. That's what I said, folks. It's wild, it's insane, it's Middle American Fantasyland. In the second part of our show, we'll feature another far-out family, when we explore the issue of transsexual fathers and their children. Who knows what's next? Transsexual mothers? Role-switching? Hey, anything can happen these days. It's crazy, it's exciting . . . and it's our show for today, so stay with us. We'll be right back."

The theme music came up as the picture went to a wide shot of the studio and stayed there. I guessed that this is where the stations were supposed to insert the first commercial. Okay. Fine.

So we sat there for a minute or two. Marsten disappeared off the set. Technicians bustled and busied some more. Then the commercial slot was over and the theme music faded. Deveaux got into position at the last second, now stationing himself midway between the set and the audience.

"The tabloids are full of aliens. There's one that visits our president regularly, if you believe tabloids. But the question here today is, do you believe your neighbors? Meet the Hayes family—"

Deveaux read from a teleprompter under the camera.

"Let's see, we have Nathan, Cheryl, Drew, and Lori Hayes, from . . . Keensville . . . no, that's Keynesville, Ohio. Right?"

"Uh . . . I'm not a Hayes," Nathan said.

"And . . ." Deveaux did a take. "I'm sorry?"

"My name is Nathan Ziegler. Cheryl and I aren't married."

"Oh, I see. But you live at the Hayes home?"

"Yes."

"With the kids?"

"Yes. I've always said that I think we're closer than most married people."

"How's that, Nathan?"

"Well, we're doing something that's not approved of. Living together, with her kids, kids from another marriage. We're flaunting society's norms, you know? And that means we have to be all the more supportive and . . . you know, caring."

"That makes sense, and you are to be congratulated for flaunting—or flouting, whichever is appropriate—society's normative values, and all that. But that isn't what the show's about today. Today, we want to talk about your extended family. More specifically, the other . . . people who live with you. If you can call them people."

"Uh-huh," Nathan said and nodded his head.

"Do you know who I mean?" Deveaux asked leadingly.

Nathan just smiled, the way he does, sort of half-humorously, half-sheepishly.

"The aliens are who I'm talking about," Deveaux said finally.

"Okay." Nathan was still nodding. "Okay."

"Now, you do have aliens living with you, do you not?"

"Uh . . . yeah. We do."

"And these are space aliens, are they not? Aliens. From another world, another galaxy."

Nathan hesitated. There seemed to be something going on inside his mind.

I was looking at him, wondering what he was going to say, here, now, on national television.

"Yes, they're space aliens."

I was amazed. Why had he picked this moment to admit it?

Then he looked worried—for a second or two, anyway.

"Well," Deveaux said. "Why don't you tell us about it? But first let me introduce—"

He let the audience know who Wayne Milburn and Trafford Starnes were, and then he asked Mom to start off telling about our family UFO experience.

What impressed me about this way of imparting information to the public is the matter of compression. Everything has to be related in the proverbial twenty-five words or less. Everything is done in "sound bites," little snippets of information, encapsulated in a few sentences, the fewer the better.

Mom started off telling about why we were going up to Pennsylvania, backgrounding the story, but Deveaux rushed her through that to the crux.

"So, let's cut to the chase here," Deveaux said. "You were driving back from picking up Nathan, and—what, this UFO buzzed your car?"

"Yeah, that's what happened," she said, shrugging.

"And what did it do?"

"Well, first it was just a bright light in the sky, and then it grew and grew, and then it started . . . you know, like, chasing us all over the place—"

"It *chased* you?"

"Yes."

"And you tried to avoid it. You were driving, Cheryl, right?"

"Right."

"You were driving. Were you scared?"

"Well, not at first, but when . . . you know, I was saying to Nathan that I had this strange feeling . . . that was before, when we picked him up . . . of course, before I left the house I had this strange feeling—you know, like, something really weird was going to happen, but Nathan always says—"

"Are you psychic, Cheryl?"

Mom giggled. "Well, not really—I mean, I don't really know. I *think* I've had some psychic experiences, like the time—"

"We'll get to those on another show. Drew, were you scared?"

"Yup," I said.

"Lori?"

"I nearly peed my pants," Lori said.

This indiscretion interrupted the fast flow of data. The audience howled, and Lori's face turned a beet red. She hadn't meant to put it quite that way.

Deveaux seemed to enjoy Lori's discomfort more than the gaffe. "So . . ." He chuckled. "So, the car is chasing you, there's this thing up there—what did it look like?"

"It was just a bright light," I said.

"So this thing, you don't know what, is up there, and it's buzzing you and you're peeing your pants—"

The audience broke up.

"—and you're afraid . . . Nathan, what's going through your mind? By the way, why weren't you driving?"

Nathan crossed his legs. I noticed that he was wearing sandals again, black sandals with black socks. "Well, I feel that this male thing about driving all the time, you know . . . that the man HAS to drive, or else he's . . . something . . . you know—"

"It's not macho to be a passenger. Is that it? If you don't drive, you're a wimp, a wuss . . . a—what?"

"Right, it's a macho thing. So, I let Cheryl drive a lot. Actually, she's a much better driver than I am. I've never been such a great driver, but that's my . . . you know, my individual—"

"Right, so you weren't driving," Deveaux rushed on, "and you see this thing . . . and what were you thinking?"

"Well, I was . . . you know . . . wondering what this thing was—but I sort of knew it . . . well, it might be a

UFO . . . but I was actually thinking that maybe it was—"

"Wayne!" Deveaux suddenly announced. "Wayne Milburn, you're the saucer guy. Did these people see a UFO?"

"Well, uh . . ."

Wayne looked a little nervous, too.

"I mean, you hear about this stuff"—Deveaux forged ahead—"you read about it, practically every week on the wire services there are stories like this, though they don't make the news every day . . . Wayne, tell me something, is all this some sort of mass psychosis, some kind of group delusion that we're all sharing . . . well, I don't know about all of us—I've never seen a UFO, much less have aliens come and use my condo like it was a Holiday Inn—By the way, Hayes family, are you charging the aliens any room and board?"

We all shook our heads.

"Wayne, so tell us, is there anything to all this . . . stuff?"

Wayne cleared his throat before stammering, "Uh, well, you see, this is a big subject . . . I've been . . . well, all my life, you see—"

"It's all nonsense!"

Deveaux had been stalking the set like a lion. But now he whirled on Trafford Starnes. He pointed a finger at him.

"Nonsense! So says Trafford Starnes. I'm glad to hear it, Mr. Starnes. Can I call you Trafford?"

"My friends call me Traf."

"Traf, listen, you're a sci-fi writer, you've done what—how many books?"

"Thirty-two."

"Thirty-two books. Novels?"

"Most of 'em, but a couple are story collections, and one or two nonfiction."

"Right, so you make your living—you do make a living?"

"Yeah, marginally." Traf chuckled.

"Marginally. Why, what with Star Trek and Star Wars and whatnot, you'd think you'd make a good buck at this kind of thing."

"I'm not Gene Roddenberry. Besides, he's dead."

"Okay, you're the sci-fi guy, and you say it's nonsense. What's with you, Traf? I thought you'd be on their side of the issue. Don't you believe in little green men?"

The audience tittered.

Starnes chuckled amiably. "It's like this. I don't believe most saucer accounts, alien visitations, whatever, for one very good, gut-level reason."

"Yeah, and what's that?"

"Because it reads like bad science fiction."

"That's marvelous. It reads like bad science fiction. What do you have to say to that, Cheryl?"

"Well, I never read science fiction. Drew, here, reads just about everything."

"Drew? By the way, Drew, you're how old again?"

"Thirteen."

"Thirteen. Did you see some bad science fiction out there, or did you see a real thing?"

"Mr. Starnes ought to know about bad science fiction," I said. "He's written enough of it."

The audience roared.

Starnes laughed, too. "The kid's quick with a comeback."

Deveaux was loving it. "Oh, it's starting to heat up. I thought we'd get through this segment without fireworks, but it looks like we're gonna have some. Okay, let's leave the literary criticism to one side, Drew. Why don't you go on with the story?"

So, I did. I spilled just about everything except the flarning. I didn't think the world was ready for flarning yet, much less vlomming. Definitely not vlomming. Anyway, it all came out, or most of it did.

"And so Zorg and . . . what's the other one's name?"

"Flez."

"So Zorg and Flez are still living with you, still up in that spare bedroom . . ."

"And in the crawlspace."

"Still up in the crawlspace, and they're parking their ship up there, too. Is that right?"

"That's right."

Deveaux was just about standing over me then. He looked down. He was very tall and just a little intimidating.

"Drew?"

"Yeah?" I said.

"You either have the biggest active imagination in history, or you're on to something very big."

"Uh-huh."

"Of course, there's another possibility, Drew. One not so nice."

"Uh-huh," I said.

"You know what it is?"

"Uh, no, sir."

"The other possibility is that you're lying."

"But I'm not. I'm not lying. It's the truth."

"You know, Drew, I don't believe you're lying."

"You don't?"

"No, I don't. I don't believe that's one of the possibilities. I think you're sincere. I think you've seen something, and I think it's captured your imagination and maybe it's carried you away a little bit. But I do believe you're sincere. But how am I going to know if you're telling the truth? You tell me, Drew."

"Have the aliens on the show," I told him.

Deveaux laughed. "Do they have an agent?"

"No. But maybe they'd agree to do it. I don't know, though. I can't speak for them."

"Well, I'll talk about it with my producer—Hal? Is Hal around? Hal, can we get the aliens on the show?"

Hal Estermann yelled something but I couldn't make it out. Some of the audience heard it and laughed.

"Okay, we'll look into it, Drew," Deveaux said, half-seriously. "Now, let's get back to the fireworks. Wayne, how long have you been investigating this saucer thing?"

Wayne barely got started before it was time for another commercial. I sat there and stewed. This was not going well.

The rest of the segment was devoted to a one-sided debate between Starnes and Milburn, punctuated with questions from the audience. Starnes, it seemed, had a degree in sociology and offered a number of theories to explain UFO sightings and attendant phenomena.

". . . not only all of that, but there's another factor."

"What's that?"

"Well, we live in a fantasyland. The public is gullible. We've been lied to for years by the government, the White House, the big corporations, and the CIA, and people have learned to distrust them. So they've come up with all this fantasy material about aliens and zombie Elvis Presleys and Bigfoot and all sorts of phantasmagoria—"

"Wow, that's a mouthful, 'phantasmagoria.' Go on, go on."

"Yeah, and so Middle America has worked up this elaborate mythology, and it's kind of attractive, it's fun, it's exciting. It's mostly untruth, but it's better than the untruth that the big multinational corporations put out, all the propaganda, all the disinformation. Actually, some of this stuff might even come from the corporations."

"It comes from the corporations?"

"Sure, maybe."

"For the purpose of—?"

"Distracting us from the big truths, like how the environment is being wrecked and how we're all being exploited and controlled, and—"

"The CIA has been covering up Bigfoot for decades," Wayne Milburn interjected.

Deveaux ignored him. "Okay, you're saying that all these saucers and things, and I guess the live-in aliens, and God knows what else—"

"The new religion," said Starnes.

"Religion?"

"In the sense that it's the opiate of the masses. It takes the place of religion."

"That's interesting, that's very interesting. You know, I must say that, while I didn't have much of an opinion about sci-fi writers before—"

"We don't like that, by the way."

"Sorry? Don't like what?"

" 'Sci-fi.' "

"You don't? I thought that was the designated, you know . . ."

"We prefer to abbreviate it as SF."

"SF? Just SF? Wait, isn't that San Francisco? [Laughter] Anyway, I haven't known many SF writers—I think we we're trying to get George Lucas on the show—but we . . . Hal? Is that true? Were we—?"

"He couldn't be bothered," Hal Estermann said, to the delight of the audience.

"He couldn't be bothered, but let me say this, Traf, you're a very intelligent and articulate man, and I thank you for being on the show, you've contributed greatly to the discussion. And now I think we have the first phone-in question. Go ahead . . . who is this—? Darlene, from Keokuk, Iowa. Hello, Darlene, are you there?"

"Yes?"

"Darlene, is that you?"

"Yes. Deveaux?"

"Go ahead, ma'am, you're on the air."

"Oh, thank you. I just want to say that I enjoy the show tremendously, and I watch it every single day."

"Thank you very much, Darlene. Your question?"

"Well, a few months ago, I began to see these lights up in the sky, and somehow . . . I don't know just how, but they seemed to be talking to me. . . ."

And so forth.

Needless to say, the rest of the show went downhill from there.

Chapter 13

I've been reading over this narrative, and parts of it amuse me. Mostly the early parts, of course, written well before the "smart drugs" took effect. I'm writing this after the effects have peaked. I now have no more pills to take.

Will I lose everything I've learned? I've learned rapidly, more rapidly than seems possible, absorbing vast amounts of undifferentiated stuff. I can still read most books in one sitting, in about half an hour. And I'm not talking about a relaxing genre novel; I mean a hefty tome, a textbook, a volume of the *Britannica*, something on that order.

Of course, I've had little time to process and order all this new data. It all must mean something, taken as a whole. I can't imagine what, but am eager to find out.

But will I lose it all, now? I don't think I can face that.

I'm writing this after certain momentous events have taken place. I've made a decision, and I must abide by it. I just hope I don't lose it all. Not everything. Let me retain something, something of this vast remodeling job that's been done on my 13-year-old brain.

Well, on with the story.

• • •

The only thing good to come out of the talk show appearance was the slip of paper, tucked in my jacket pocket, with Kristina's address and phone number on it. Of course there was the little matter of 800 miles. The problem wasn't so much the distance as it was my showing up at Kristina's door with no believable explanation for how I got there.

Then again, I had a flying saucer at my disposal, and everyone in the world knew about it. Why, on second thought, would my sudden appearance many miles from home be unexplainable?

Still, it would be awkward. I was no 13-year-old Don Juan. I was more like the character Christien, in *Cyrano de Bergerac*. Tongue-tied at the very sight of a woman.

Well, not exactly tongue-tied. I hadn't exactly been that at the studio, had I? No. But I was no smoothie, either.

Okay.

The next night, I called Kristina's number, desperately hoping that she'd answer and not either of her mothers.

One ring . . . two . . . three . . . four . . .

It looked as though no one would answer. My heart sank a little. Maybe they hadn't come home yet. Maybe they got a chance to go into New York. I was envious of anyone who'd seen it from the ground.

Five . . . six . . .

"Hello?"

"Kristina?"

"Yes?"

"Hi, this is Drew Hayes."

"Drew! How nice to hear from you. We just got back, maybe a half-hour ago. I'm pooped."

"Am I calling at a bad time? I can call back."

"No! That's okay, really. I'm glad you called."

You know, I really liked this girl. She was always so friendly. I like that in a person.

"So, what's up, Drew?"

"Uh, not a lot. I went back to school today, and everyone was in a fit about us being on TV. Everyone saw it."

"Uh-oh, I haven't been back yet," Kristina said. "I sort of thought that kind of thing would happen."

"Does it bother you?"

"Does what?"

"Oh, you know, about what the kids think about your dad, and all."

"No, not really. I mean, they don't understand. They're kind of ignorant, they don't know . . . you know . . ."

"Uh-huh. Well, I hope you don't have a hard time."

"Thanks. Hope you don't either."

"Oh, I'm used to it. They talk about us all the time. Mrs. Carey across the street spies on us."

"Nosy neighbors, huh? We have 'em, too."

"Yeah. Say, look, Kristina."

"Yeah?"

"How about going out with me some time?"

"Uh . . . okay. Yeah, sure. I'd like that. I don't know if my parents would let me, but I'd like to."

"You've never been on a date?"

"No. Have you?"

"No."

"Oh."

"But, you know, it doesn't have to be a date. I just want to see you."

"Yeah. That'd be nice. But . . ."

"Yeah, I know, we live far apart."

"I'll say. Don't you live in Ohio?"

"Yeah. I know it's far. But, you see, I can come to Minneapolis."

"You can?" Kristina was amazed. "Wow, that'd be really cool! When?"

"How about tonight?"

"Huh?"

"Hello?"

"Yeah, I'm here. Did you say tonight?"

"Yeah, I said tonight. Why, is that a problem?"

"No, not really. How are you going to get here? Are you going to fly out?"

"Yeah."

"Really? Why are you coming to Minneapolis?"

"To visit relatives."

"No kidding! Wow, this is really great. I never thought . . . yeah, so when are you coming?"

"Uh, about midnight. Central Time."

"Midnight? Jeez."

"I know it's late. Actually, it might be later."

"But . . . I mean, I'll be in bed."

"Can you wait up for me?"

"But . . . Drew, I don't know."

"I'll knock on your bedroom window."

"What?"

"Where's your bedroom. Second floor?"

"Yeah. But how in the world are you going to knock on my bedroom window?"

"With my knuckles. What side of the house?"

"What do you mean, what side of the . . . ? Drew, are you kidding me, or what?"

"I'm not kidding," I said sincerely as I could manage. "From the front, what side of the house is your bedroom on?"

"The right side."

"Right side, second floor."

"It's on the right rear corner of the second floor."

"Okay, that's easy. I'll see you about midnight, or maybe a little after."

"Are you going to come in? I don't know if my parents would like—"

"No, I'm going to pick you up."

"Really? In what?"

"In my flying saucer."

There was a long silence. I thought the line had gone dead.

"Kristina?"

"I'm here."

"Did you hear what I said?"

"Yeah."

"Do you believe me?"

"Yeah."

She'd said it as if she believed it.

"Wow," she said.

"Yeah. I wasn't fooling about the aliens, you know."

"I guess you weren't."

"Are you sure you believe me?"

She didn't answer for a moment. Then: "Yes, I believe you. But you better not be fooling me. If you say you're going to pick me up in a flying saucer, you'd better do it, or I'll never speak to you again."

"Right. I'll be there. Don't fall asleep."

"Are you kidding? I wouldn't miss this for the world."

"Okay, then. See you tonight."

"See you."

"Bye."

"Bye."

At about 11:30 Eastern Standard Time I got dressed in jacket, sneakers, and jeans, made sure Tyler was asleep, and went out into the hallway. I walked past Mom's room. She was asleep. Nathan, I was fairly sure, was down in the basement, hard at work at his computer. He had begun a novel, he said, about his experiences in the Peace Corps. He'd done a stint in Ethiopia in the early nineteen-seventies.

"A novel?" I'd asked.

"Yeah, sort of autobiographical."

"Great," I said. "Have a working title?"

"Well, no, not yet." Nathan put his feet up on the oak-veneered desk. "You've been doing a lot of writing yourself lately, haven't you?"

I nodded. "Yeah, sort of."

"About Zorg and Flez?"

"Yeah. About . . . you know, the strangeness of it all."

"Yeah." Nathan nodded slowly. "I really don't understand it very well myself."

Sure you don't, I wanted to tell him. You've been influenced, if not downright manipulated. Aliens have put strange thoughts in your brain.

And they had. It was Kel's engineering, of course. I had an idea of how it was done—tightly focused electromagetic fields, which set up certain inductances inside the human brain. I don't think they could have made zombies out of us, but they certainly influenced our behavior. As I look at it now, they took advantage of certain predispositions. Certainly they did with Nathan, who tends, I think, to lack a capacity for skepticism. Nathan has given himself whole-heartedly to cause after cause, but I don't believe he's done much thinking about any of them. Oh, to a certain degree he has, of course, and he is by no means thick-witted or easily gulled. He simply finds the plight of the underdog irresist-ible and follows that rubric when ordering his moral priorities. If a certain ideology or political posture declaims on behalf of the poor, the oppressed, the put-upon, he's for it. If not, not. The trouble with this approach is that it produces a kind of moral myopia, a shortsightedness that can see intentions well enough, but which has trouble focusing on methods and results that could cast doubt on those intentions.

I knocked softly against the aliens' bedroom door.

There was no answer, but I knew they were in.

As always, the door was unlocked. I eased it open and looked in. The two saucer occupants weren't in sight. I stepped in and closed the door.

The room was lighted, as always. It had grown a bit crowded in here lately. Piles of games, toys, comic books, magazines, computer programs, and video tapes rose almost hip-high. Racks of video and audio equipment covered three walls. Nathan had installed some of it, but it looked as though other hands had been at work. Zorg and Flez? Or Kel, through some mechanical medium? I didn't know.

I stepped gingerly through the mess, looking behind ad hoc walls constructed of stacks of comic books. I finally saw that both of them were in the room, flat on their backs, each ensconced inside a miniature fortress of audio components, stacks of CDs, and general debris. They never had moved upstairs.

They looked asleep, but Zorg immediately opened one eye.

"Hey."

He sat up.

"Hi, Zorg. Sorry about breaking in on you, but I wanted to ask a favor."

"Sure."

"Could we flarn tonight?"

Flez had sat up, too. "Dude!"

"Hi, Flez. Uh—"

"He wants to flarn, dude."

"All *right!*"

"Great," I said, "but I have a specific location in mind. I mean . . . well, what I mean is, I want to pick up a girl."

Zorg looked at Flez, and Flez looked at Zorg.

"All riiiight!"

Chapter 14

I don't know when I began to divine exactly how the aliens spent most of their time. They were exceedingly quiet and kept to themselves; in point of fact, for most of their four-month stay, they barely intruded into our collective consciousness. Nathan stopped taking them out driving after a few weeks. After that, we hardly knew they were there, and it never occurred to anyone but me to ask what the heck they were doing up there in the spare bedroom all the time, besides reading comic books and playing video games.

They weren't, really; at least the games and toys were only part of it.

It dawned on me only gradually that what has now come to be called "virtual reality" had a lot to do with what was going on, and that Kel, the ship, provided the means to create this reality. For the truth was that Zorg and Flez spent most of their time flat on their backs, zonked out, their brains interlocked—or interfaced, to use current tech lingo—with Kel, which was in essence a highly advanced computer, or some contrivance totally beyond computers.

What did they do in this dreamlike state? I had only an inkling. They played games, perhaps, indulged in elaborate fantasies, became anything they wanted to be. They viewed endless movies, "interactive" narratives in which the viewer participates, even to the extent of playing the leading characters. They solved puzzles, relived moments of their particular race's history. . . .

It could have been that they were in communication with others or their species all over the galaxy, or beyond, hooked into some vast computer supernetwork. The possibilities were limitless, given the astonishing level of technology which Kel, the ship, represented.

How did all the Earth-derived games and pastimes figure in? I suppose it was all grist for their mill, fresh material, new thrills, new kicks.

Or. . . .

Another explanation occurred to me. Could Z. & F. be . . . for lack of a better term, *anthropologists*, serious investigators into what were, to them, alien creatures, mores, and ways of doing things? (I think the word *culture* has been corrupted a bit by our anthropologists. It used to mean refinement, art, learning, that sort of thing, and now means what we used to mean by *civilization*. But let that pass.)

Zorg and Flez—academicians? Scientists, gathering data for a doctoral dissertation? Serious researchers?

"Let's flarn, dudes!"

"Yeah!"

The lights of Chicago moved below. The Sears Tower thrust itself up like a Christmas tree designed by Mies van der Rohe.

"Can we pick up the girl first?" I asked. "Then we'll flarn."

"Fer sure, dude," Flez said.

I couldn't remember when they'd started using current slang, though their speech had always been colloquial. They'd no doubt been watching lots of MTV.

Sometimes, while flarning, they'd play rock music. That

is, they'd let me hear it, if I asked for it. Usually I didn't, preferring to take in the sights in silence.

"Zorg, tell me something. Is there anyplace else in the universe that has rock 'n' roll music?"

"Nope. This is it, as far as we know."

I nodded.

"Do you guys have a map of Minneapolis?"

"Sure do."

I watched the bulkhead. There it was, something more than a map. It was a three-dimensional computer model, an astonishingly detailed simulacrum of the entire city and environs, down to the infrastructure. Not only could I see exactly where Kristina's street was; it was far better than that. At her precise address there was an approximation of her house.

Was this a standard map, one among many, or had Zorg and Flez created it? Either way, it was an astounding artifact.

These aliens knew so much about us. Had it been on their agenda to invade and conquer, we would have been sitting ducks. Thankfully, they did not have such an agenda.

The exurban electric grid sprawled below, moving off to the east. A few moments later the lines of light dispersed into rural reticulations. Then, darkness.

"Can we go faster?" I asked.

"Sure, if you want to."

"He's in a hurry," Flez said.

"How'd you meet her?" Zorg asked.

"On the TV show. Did you see us?"

They chortled.

"I guess you did," I said. "Pretty silly, wasn't it?"

"Fer sure," Flez said. "Major airheads."

"World-class bone brains, dude," Zorg said.

I sighed. "Yeah, but that's humanity."

"Yeah, we know," Zorg said. "That's why we like it."

They both giggled.

"Yeah? Okay, if you say so."

Hard to guess what they meant here. They did seem to like Earth and Earthians. Earthlings.

I smiled.

Earthlings, prepare to meet your doom. . . .

No, things weren't working out as they did in B sci-fi flicks. But then the movie was still running, wasn't it? Sometimes I thought I could smell popcorn.

Suburban Minneapolis lay below. Off to the east, a few miles away, a net of light that was St. Paul.

"Almost there, dude," Zorg said.

I looked down. The ground was getting closer. When we did this, floating over cities, I got nervous. I was very nervous now.

"Zorg, can't anybody see us down there?"

"Sure, why not?"

"But, don't you have stealth capability?"

"Huh? Oh, yeah. Sure."

"How come you don't use it?"

"Hey, that wouldn't be good flarn, dude."

Good flarn. Scare the locals, stir things up. Fun. But the locals seemed mostly to ignore us. What about radar, the ultrasensitive national air defense system? I eventually concluded that after so many years of UFO flaps, after tens of thousands of reports and investigations and swarms of blips on radar scopes, today's military air detection systems are programmed to ignore UFO's unless they shape up to be threatening. You see a splotch on the screen that's hurtling along at something like Mach 6, and it doesn't look like a missile, and it sure as hell isn't a plane, and you say, well, so what? There's another UFO. Some kind of radar shadow, a fluke of temperature inversion, a moon reflection . . . who can say, and anyway, who cares? You tell your computer to ignore it, and the ghostly blip disappears from your screen.

An old two-story house hulked below. The ship floated over the back yard.

"That window, there. See? Second floor."

"Right," Flez said.

The window was lighted. I looked at my watch. It was about ten till midnight, Central Time.

"Okay, let's wait a minute," I said.

I watched the window. It wasn't long before Kristina—I could see her well—appeared at the window.

Her jaw dropped.

"Okay, go down slowly," I said.

The ship descended, edging toward the house.

"Can you open up a door in the top part of the ship?" I asked Flez.

"Anywhere."

"Good."

I got up and took a few steps, reached up and touched the dome overhead. It was soft to the touch.

"About there?"

"Sure, dude."

That section of hull was opaque. It now became transparent and I could see the window. Kristina, in a pink sweatshirt, stared out at us. The transparency was one way, though.

A wide hole dilated in the ship's ultrathin skin. Now she could see me. I waved. She waved and lifted the bottom half of the double-hung window. Her face was flushed with excitement.

"I don't *believe* this!" she squealed.

"Shhh!" I ducked down to talk to Zorg. "Can you get right under the window? Don't bump the house."

"Sure thing, dude."

The outer edge of the saucer-shaped craft kissed siding. I poked my head up through the hole.

"Kristina, come on!" I said in a semiwhisper.

"Will it . . . I mean, can I just—?"

"Climb through the window, that's it."

She did it, and warily put one tennis shoe down on the hull.

"Will it hold me?"

"Sure."

I reached out my hand, and she grasped it.

"Gotcha."

I pulled her through. She kept low, went to her pretty haunches. She was wearing tight, white jeans.

"Swing your legs down."

She did, and I pulled her off the hull and down through the hole. The opening closed immediately.

"Let's split, guys."

We got out of there fast. The city dropped away. Looking down through a glassy section of floor, Kristina looked stunned.

"Jeez," she said.

"Yeah, it takes some time to get used to," I said.

"I don't believe it, I really don't."

I smiled. She was wearing perfume. Which brand, I didn't know, but it smelled wonderful. She smelled wonderful. Her left ear was pierced with one simple gold loop. Her hair was on the short side but not too short. The color was a medium blond, golden, like corn. I thought she looked great.

"I didn't think you'd come," she said. "I mean, I couldn't believe it, not quite."

"No faith, huh? Well, I came."

"You sure did. This is . . ."

She turned to look at our alien pilots.

"Hey, girl," Zorg said.

"Hi, babe," Flez offered.

"Hi," Kristina said.

"Oh, yeah," I said. "Zorg, Flez, this is Kristina Peerson."

"Call me Kris."

"Hi, Kris."

"Hi, Kris, nice to meet you. You like to have fun?"

"Sure!"

"Great, babe."

I said, "Oh, and . . . yeah, you should meet Kel."

"Hello, Kris," Kel said.

"Hello?" Kris looked at me questioningly.

"Kel is the ship," I said simply.

"Oh." Then it sank in. "Oh."

"Takes some getting used to. It's a great ship, though. It can go just about anywhere."

"Where are we going?" Kris asked.

"Anywhere you want to," Zorg said.

"Like, anywhere?"

"Sure."

Kris looked at me. "You mean, for instance . . . Egypt?"

"Great place," Zorg said. "Pyramids."

"It's morning there," I said. "If you don't mind, we could go."

"Wow. I don't—Yeah, let's go."

So we went to Egypt. The flight took under fifteen minutes, our flight path a trajectory (I'm guessing) high in the stratosphere. A million stars followed us until we hit morning and the sun came up. Kel served us Coke and ice and some things like cookies, though they tasted strange. But edible.

"Wow, do we get a movie?" Kris asked.

"Yeah, *It Came From Outer Space*. Great flick, with a script by Ray Bradbury."

"He's great, I've read him."

Good taste in literature, too.

Over the Mediterranean, the ship plunged but our stomachs didn't drop out.

After some maneuvering, we were overflying Cairo, a sea of white stone buildings.

"Where are the Pyramids?" Kris wanted to know. "Aren't they out in the desert?"

"The pyramids at Giza are right on the edge of the city," I informed her. "That's where the Great Pyramid is."

"Great . . . I mean, wonderful. Was King Tut buried in one of those?"

"It would be great to see Tut's tomb, but we'd have to get out. It's way upriver, in the Valley of Kings."

"Does he have a pyramid?"

"No. Tut's reign was more than a millennium after the era of pyramid-building."

"You know a lot about Egypt."

I'll admit I was showing off a bit. I decided to cool it. I didn't need to do it. If ever a young man had impressed a young lady, I had done it, was doing it. Who wouldn't be absolutely floored by it all? Even I hadn't quite accustomed myself to living in Zorg and Flez's universe.

Kris leaned toward me and whispered, "They look like . . ."

"Yeah, I know."

Actually, to me they had changed, very subtly. They looked a tad less human. The eyes were alien, different. I could see odd little markings on their noses and foreheads. Their fingers seemed oddly slender. Nothing jumped out at you, but signs and hints were there.

I'd often wondered, of course, if they had disguised their real appearance. I had come to believe they had, and sometimes speculated as to what they really looked like. Visions of the obligatorily tentacled type came to me every so often. But in these aliens' advanced technological milieu, what was "real" and what was not? Simple matter, to engineer their bodies to look human or quasihuman, and do so permanently. They could probably reproduce that way if they wanted to.

Reproduction. Every once in a while I was amazed by what I didn't know about them and never thought of asking. I put it down to mind control.

We hovered over the Great Pyramid, a mountain of cracked, weathered stone sitting timelessly in bright morning light. At its base huddled the attendant ruined necropolis with its lesser pyramids. The Sphinx, silent as ever, crouched nearby.

"This is . . . oh, this is so *great*."

Kris shook her head in wonderment.

The Nile was a ribbon of blue. We toured the sights all the way upriver to Karnak, but, because of the low sun, the interior of the ancient many-columned temple was steeped in gloom, and although Flez offered to shine a light down on it, I declined.

"We'll attract attention. This is crazy," I said. "Let's go to the other side of the . . . wait."

Kris, Flez, and Zorg regarded me as I thought it over.

Finally I said, "Let's go to Mars."

Chapter 15

It didn't take a super IQ to notice that Zorg and Flez were complete morons, albeit morons by choice, not chance. Yet they commanded a vessel that was a technological miracle. How could this be?

Well, that's easy. You don't have to be a computer whiz to run a computer. And at this hyperadvanced level of technological development, you could pilot a star ship while indulging in the mindless diversion of your choice.

The wider question was this: obviously Zorg and Flez were smarter than they let on. But did their race create Kel and his ilk, or were they just users? I gave this a lot of thought, but couldn't decide. Could those dumb pills be powerful enough to reduce surpassing genius to mindless thrill-seeking?

I shuddered to think that I might have taken the pills myself. Ye gods, what would the effect have been? I might have ended up in Special Ed., or worse. Institutionalized.

Who wants to be dumb? Why would anyone deliberately reduce his intelligence?

"Want to get stupid?"

Getting stupid: the pastime of choice among advanced alien races.

• • •

Kris looked at me in awed disbelief.

"M-m . . . Mars?"

"Yup."

"We're *really* going all the way to *Mars*?"

"Yeah. Why, don't you want to?"

"Well, yeah . . . I guess. But I have to be back home by—"

"Don't worry, it will take only an hour or so to get there. An hour back, maybe. Right, Zorg?"

"Right."

Kris settled back in the chair Kel had conjured up for her. She shook her head. "Mars."

"I want to get a look at that so-called face," I said.

"The what?"

"Surface formation that some people swear looks like a face."

"Oh, that. I was reading about it. Do you think there once could have been people on Mars?"

"No," I said. "But I guess you can't rule it out entirely. Anyway, we'll get a close look at it. If we can find it. Flez, go you have a Martian map?"

"Sure do, dude."

I smiled at Kris. "They have everything."

She laughed. "I'll say!"

But an hour is a long time to just sit there. There's not much to look at in deep space, besides stars, which get old pretty quick.

"Zorg, do you have anything we can do?"

"Sure. Movies? Games?"

"Uh . . . what kind of games?"

"Earth games. Or our games."

"What are your games like?"

"You probably won't like them."

"Kris, do you want to play one of Zorg's games?"

She shrugged. "Sure."

"Okay, Zorg. We'll play."

We played one of Zorg's games, and he was absolutely right. It wasn't for us.

It's hard to describe what real, total virtual reality is like. The reality of the ship didn't disappear, wasn't supplanted by the virtual reality. There were two realities.

I did tell you this was hard to explain.

Now, to get to the "game." It had something to do with knocking multicolored shapes about. You pushed one into another and made something, then you knocked that thing into another thing . . .

I knew this would be hard, but I didn't think it would be impossible. I mean, it was an okay game, don't get me wrong. And there was a lot more to it than that. I wasn't intellectual, though. It wasn't a puzzle. It didn't make you think, but you had to be fast, you had to react. I guess it was like one of our video games, only it was different.

We had to stop playing because Kris really did not understand it or disliked it too intensely to learn. I didn't mind. It wasn't to my liking either.

"How about a movie?"

"Okay," Kris said.

"Zorg?"

"Okay. You'll like this one."

We watched the "movie." It was an alien movie. It didn't make much sense, and I think the story was set on Zorg and Flez's world. It was a pretty world of tall transparent buildings and green meadows. People much like Zorg and Flez moved through it, working, playing, eating, sleeping, just like humans. These creatures were a little different, though. They did not look human, not very much, but they did have a head, a trunk, two upper and two lower appendages. In other words, they were humanoid. They did not look like any actor. They were bald on top, though, and had long, stringy hair on the sides of their head.

Anyway, it was an interesting movie. I have no idea what it was about, even though there were English subtitles. The dialogue was . . . well, "archly poetic," I think, is the phrase I'm looking for. Or "nonsensical," maybe. Surreal? Postmodern. I dunno, my reading in those areas is spotty. Give me a break, I've only had three months to become a literary genius.

So we went to Mars. It was great, though it got boring quickly. Endless miles of desolation. Pretty desolation, granted. The Valles Marineris was impressive, I'll have to admit. Has the Grand Canyon beat all to heck. On the other hand, Olympus Mons, the biggest shield volcano in the solar system, was just an oversize mountain.

There were vast areas of absolute nothingness, undifferentiated badlands. These were a colossal bore. I don't know that Mars would be all that interesting a place to live. How unlike Earth it was. There was a sameness and uniformity that Earth thankfully doesn't have. Our home world is an endlessly varied, endlessly interesting place.

We found Viking Lander 2. It looked anomalous, so obviously an artifact set in a landscape untouched by human or alien hands. It sat there, lonely but brave, on the surface of a distant alien world. It would never return home—until the day that men would come to Mars, perhaps. Maybe then it would be shipped back home to its final resting place in the Smithsonian Air and Space Museum.

Would men ever come to Mars? The way things are going, it doesn't look likely. But hope springs eternal, and all that.

We couldn't find the "face." It wasn't marked on the map, which leads me to believe that it was just a fluke of shadow or a glitch in the Viking Orbiter's scanning program.

The thing that most impressed me about the terrain was the number of craters. Parts of Mars look almost like the Moon, when viewed from a high enough vantage point. There were craters of all sizes, ranging from ones a few yards wide to a few that gaped for miles.

It was in one of the middle-sized ones that Blog was hiding, lying in wait for us.

"DUDE!"

Zorg saw it first. Flez jumped and twisted around.

"Uh-oh!"

I looked. It was a ship, rising out of a deep crater. A big ship, much bigger than Kel.

"Oh, look," Kris said casually. "Who is it?"

I was really scared. Not for myself, but for Kris. I silently berated myself for the foolishness of coming all the way out here. I had to impress the girl.

One of Mom's favorite phrases is "testosterone poisoning." It generally means, I think, that males have their own built-in stupid drug. I can't say that the notion doesn't have some credence. Many a man has been done in by excessive zeal in the eternal pursuit of woman.

But Kris was in danger, too.

Kel, the ship, leapt up at the pink Martian sky, gaining altitude faster than it seemed possible to do. The planet fell away vertiginously.

"Who was that?" Kris asked again.

"I don't really know," I said.

"Blog, man." Zorg shook his bald head. "Bummer."

"Blog?" Kris shrugged. "Another alien?"

"I suppose so," I said. "Though probably not kin to Zorg and Flez."

I was talking mainly to keep from screaming. Terror was beginning to rise in me. I think I could have faced it alone. But the guilt engendered by Kris's being there made the situation almost unbearable.

"Zorg, can we lose Blog?"

"Maybe, dude."

The red disk of Mars receded as if in an animated NASA film. We shot through the surrounding starry globe of space, racing sunward.

"Is Borg after us?" Kris asked.

"Probably."

"Fer sure," Flez said. "Gaining."

I let out a breath. Damn. I wanted to ask if Kel could

outrun Blog, but didn't want to distract our pilots from their tasks. That is, if they truly had tasks and weren't just along for the ride like us.

"Gaining!" Flez sounded really worried now.

"Bummer," Zorg said. He looked at his partner.

"Should we, dude?"

Flez answered immediately, "Do it, dude."

Zorg nodded. "Yeah."

Kel's voice was firm. "It is highly inadvisable to make transference in close proximity to sizable concentrations of mass."

I gathered Kel was talking about the sun, and not Mars, because Mars was lost in our space dust.

"Don't be a wuss, Kel," Flez said.

"Do it, Kel," Zorg ordered.

"Dorks," Kel said. "You asked for it."

Something strange happened. The Earth appeared out of nowhere in front of us. We rushed to meet it.

Kris jumped a little. "Whew! How did that happen?"

"I don't know. I guess that was a hyperspace transition."

"Right."

She seemed to understand it. I guess everyone these days has an inkling as to what faster-than-light travel is all about. But who really can explain it? What exactly does "hyperspace" mean? Or "subspace" or any of those handy sci-fi coinages. I thought I had a fairly good idea, but when I question myself, I find that the entire notion is rather slippery. I read a scientific paper about wormholes recently. They make a lot more sense than either of those first two ideas. At least Einstein thought so.

Call it what you will, though, the end result was the same. We had just crossed millions of miles of space in an instant.

"Whoa, dude!"

The planet's surface was coming up fast. I was seized with a fear that we'd burn up in the atmosphere, like some wayward meteorite. Someone down there would happen to

glance up and see us, a streak of fire across the sky, brief
and brilliant. And that would be it for us.

But it didn't happen. For a short time a faint yellow glow
surrounded the ship, but that was all. The reentry was
smooth. We were coming in over a vast body of water, the
Pacific, from the looks of it. But quick to come up was land,
laid out like California, though no sprawling urban concentrations were visible, so we couldn't have been near Los
Angeles. Good thing, because I estimated our speed at
around Mach 8. Whew! That was almost impossible at the
altitude we were at. Well, no, it was possible, because it was
happening. We'd have broken every window in L.A.

On second thought, if you believe the reports, saucers
don't usually make sonic booms, no matter what speed they
travel. I had no idea if Kel left a sonic wake or not.

It was dark, still night. I looked at my watch. It was a few
minutes before 3, Eastern Time. I hoped we could make it
across the country to Minneapolis in time to get Kris back
before her parents, who I hoped were fast asleep, knew
anything. My butt would be in the frying pan if we didn't.

But it looked as though we weren't going to try to make
it across the country. Below, in the starlight, was a terrain as
bleak any offered on Mars.

"What are we doing, guys?"

"Gonna hide out, dude," Flez said.

"Oh. Think it will do any good?"

"Maybe," Zorg said.

"Maybe not," Flez added.

A few minutes passed while the ship dodged and floated
among some low, eroded hills. I didn't quite understand
what was going on, but our alien pilots were obviously
searching for something.

No moon, dim starlight fighting to get through a thin
cloud cover, but we had light-amplification gear. I could see
everything, murky though it was. I spotted a darker area in
the face of the hill we were creeping up.

"How about it?" Zorg asked of Flez.

"Yeah, okay."

"Guys, uh, what are we going to do?"

"Get small, dude."

"Get small?"

"Yeah. Contract the ship, like, you know. Make it small. Then slip into the cave. Cool."

Oh, a cave.

Make it small?

"But, won't we . . . ?"

I couldn't bring myself to ask the obvious question. The walls started closing in.

Kris was concerned. "What's happening?"

"They can shrink the ship," I said. "Make it small. Small enough to fit into one of these caves up here."

"Holy smoke. How small?"

"I don't know."

"About twelve feet across," Flez said. "Don't worry, dude and babe."

"Okay, if you say so," I said.

The ship shrank. Our chairs melted away, receding into the floor. Soon there was nothing left to sit on.

The bulkhead came up to nudge me, and I had to move closer to Kris, which I didn't mind so much. She didn't seem to mind it either. She still smelled good, though the bloom had come off the rose. It was getting close.

The ship, now contracted to less than half its diameter, eased into the mouth of the cave. Very slowly. Whoever was at the helm was doing a fantastic job of docking.

We receded into the darkness. Presently, there came a soft bump, and the ship shuddered a bit.

"Ooops," Flez said. "Easy."

"Yeah," Zorg said. "Get smaller, dude."

The walls contracted more, squeezing us in.

We floated farther in at a snail's pace. At long last, the ship stopped and settled. The lights, except for a soft red glow coming from nowhere in particular, went out. The ship's engines died with a barely audible whine. All was quiet.

There were the four of us, two humans, two aliens, in a cramped space the size of a not-so-large packing crate.

Kris's warm breath came against my cheek.

"I'm scared," she said.

"Don't worry," I said. It was up to me to be brave. After all, I had the testosterone.

"Don't talk, dudes," Flez said.

We were quiet. Complete silence descended. The aliens sat there, as they usually did, facing each other, short legs crossed. The faint reddish light reflected off the sheen of their gabardines and turned the rococo garishness of their Hawaiian shirts into monochrome psychedelics.

A long time passed, and I spent it drinking in Kris's presence. We were close, but just barely touching. Gently, I lowered my head on her shoulder, and she did the same to me. We sat like that for a long time. Then I kissed her cheek. She turned her head slightly and her eyes found mine. We looked at each other. Then we kissed, very softly. A thrill went through me like no other.

Faint light came from the cave's entrance. It moved, which meant its source was moving.

"Bummer," Flez murmured.

The light came stronger next time, playing about the mouth of the cave. It looked like a strong searchlight beam.

"Maybe they're human," I said in Kris's ear.

"What a drag," Zorg said, and I knew it wasn't human.

The ship suddenly came to life, its engines powering up with a sharp twangy whine.

"Okay, dudes," Zorg said, "we gotta let you off. It's been nice."

"Here?" I said.

"Here, dude. It was real cool. Thanks."

"You're leaving? Going home?"

"Maybe, dude. Maybe not. We gotta go, though."

"Right," I said. "It's been fun."

"Yeah, way cool."

"Do you think you can get away from Blog?"

"Yeah, no problem. Maybe. I dunno."

"I hope you guys make it."

"Yeah, thanks, dude. Later."

The floor opened up and we floated down. There wasn't much room underneath the vessel, and we had to crouch on the rocky floor of the cave.

The ship moved off, floating away from us in the darkness, threading its way through the narrow passage.

Then strong light hit the cave's mouth, starkly outlining the ship's bulbous form.

The jig was up. We were found, or Zorg and Flez were. I pulled Kris to the smooth floor and got on top of her, shielding her from what I was afraid was about to happen. I pushed my face into Kris's soft shoulder and braced for an explosion.

But none came. I dared to look up. The ship seemed to shrink slightly. Then it gave a little quiver before it shot out of the cave like a howitzer shell. It was gone in an instant, and the light disappeared with it.

Kris and I were left in darkness.

We waited, but nothing happened. The silence returned, and all I could hear was the beating of my heart. It was going pretty good.

Finally, I rolled off Kris. She groaned, then sat up.

"I don't believe this," she said.

"Sorry I got you into it."

"Oh, that's all right. It wasn't your fault."

"Thanks."

"Do you know who Blog is?"

"No. But it has to be an enemy. Maybe another race of aliens that Zorg and Flez's people are at war with."

"Wow. How come they didn't shoot?"

"I don't know. Maybe because we were here."

"That was nice of them."

"Yeah. Boy, I hope the guys got away."

"I hope so, too," Kris said.

We sat there for a while, then we both got up.

"Jeez, my parents are going to kill me," she said.

"Mine, too," I said.

"Where are we?"

"I don't know, but I have the feeling that we're in Nevada."

"Nevada? Oh, my God, that's miles and miles away from Minnesota."

"I'm afraid we won't get back to Minnesota tonight."

"What are we going to do?"

"We can phone home."

"Do you think we can find a phone out here?"

"I don't know. I'm hoping we can find a highway. If we can find one, a phone should be within walking distance. First, though, we gotta get out of this cave."

I took her hand and we walked toward the faint oval at the end of the passage.

When we reached the entrance, I could see immediately that we had a real problem.

"Oh, my," Kris said.

"Yeah. Forget about the highway for now."

The mouth of the cave was set into the face of a sheer cliff. We were a good hundred feet above the ground.

Chapter 16

I've noticed a certain unevenness to this narrative, and I'm not talking about the pre-genius parts. Somethings I can muster a fairly good prose style; in other spots I trail off into semiliteracy again. I wonder if this is due to the wearing off of the drugs (or "effectuators," as Kel called them). Maybe it's because the drugs are alien in origin and aren't meant for humans. I wanted to talk to Kel about this, but didn't find the time.

I still seem to be fairly intelligent. I'm not drooling into my pablum or anything. So far so good, said the man as he fell from the top of the skyscraper.

"There's no way down," Kris said in despair.

I sure didn't see any quick way down. I knelt and waited for my eyes to pick out some detail in the nearly vertical mountainside below us.

Nearly vertical, but not completely. There was a chance we could climb down. For a mediocre rock climber, with the right equipment, it would have been a breeze. But we weren't even mediocre, and we had nothing whatsoever in the way of equipment. We didn't even have anything to improvise with.

Not like in the movies, where the hero just happens to have a length of rope or some gadget, carefully set up in the first reel, that does the trick. I had nothing, not so much as a rubber band or a paper clip. I didn't even have my wallet.

"I wish Zorg and Flez had given us something to get down from here," Kris said.

"They were pretty preoccupied," I said. Besides, I wanted to say, they're bloody morons.

"Yeah, you're right, I guess they were kind of busy. Anyway, what are we going to do, Drew?"

"We're going to climb down. See this ledge here?"

"Yeah. Wait a minute, you don't think I'm going to—"

"See how it slants down? It intersects with another ledge, and that one goes—do you see it?"

"No."

"Well, we're going to have to try it, or we'll be up here forever. No telling where we are. We're probably miles out in the desert. They'd never find us in a million years."

"I don't think I can do it, Drew."

I looked at the ledge again. It was barely six inches wide. I looked down. It was a long way.

"I don't think I can do it either," I said.

I got up and turned around.

"Wonder how far this cave goes back."

"Where would it go?"

"No telling," I said. "It could go back for a good ways. There are caves that are miles deep."

"We don't have a flashlight— Oh, wait!"

"What?"

Kris dug into the right hip pocket of her jeans and pulled something out. She held it up, and it jingled. "A Penlight! On the keychain. I have no idea— Wait a minute."

She fiddled with it until the end of the penlight glowed with a feeble light. But it was better than total darkness.

"All right! What a stroke of luck." I held out my hand. "Let's go."

She took my hand.

I stopped. "Are you afraid of caves?"

"No."

"Bats?"

"I don't like bats," she said. "But I'm not afraid of them. They won't bite if you don't bother them."

"Just checking. There might be bats."

"It's night. Bats go out at night."

I looked at her. "You're right. But snakes . . ."

"I like snakes," she said.

"Uh-huh. Good. Let's go."

Maybe Kris had some testosterone, too.

The cave did not go back much farther from where the ship had been. The passage reached a dead end and that was it. There was a side passage, however, very narrow, which twisted to the left. I got the notion that it might connect to another cave.

"Over here," I said.

"Where does it go?"

"One way to find out."

We sidled along for a while, me in the lead with the penlight.

The passage constricted as it turned, but it was going in the right direction, toward the mountainside, so I decided to follow it as far as we could.

"Have you ever done any caving?" Kris asked.

"Yeah, a little," I lied. "Why, have you?"

"I've been to Carlsbad Caverns."

"Hey, that's a cave."

"Yeah, but it was a guided tour. We didn't go back into the wild parts. I want to some day."

"Yeah. Well, here we are, caving."

"With no equipment."

"Right. Hey."

"What?"

I played the penlight's weak beam on something in the floor. It was the opening to a shaft.

"It goes down pretty far," I said.

Kris leaned over my shoulder. "Jeez," she said.

I nodded. "Yeah, it's scary. But it could connect up with another cave, lower down in the cliff."

"Even if it does," Kris said, "we could get lost real easy."

"You're right. Want to wait till morning and try scaling down the hillside?"

"That scares me even more."

"You afraid of heights?"

"When you can fall and kill yourself? You bet."

Sensible woman, I thought.

There were ledges and footholds along the shaft going down as far as I could see, which, of course, wasn't very far. But we had to risk it. I clenched the penlight between my teeth and started down.

It was easy for the first few feet, but then the footholds turned into toeholds, and then to cracks that you could maybe wedge the edge of your sole into.

"How is it?" Kris called.

"I think this is about as far as I can go. It's a straight drop—"

I dropped.

Next thing I knew I was at the bottom of the shaft. But I hadn't fallen very far. I landed on my butt. I wasn't hurt, at least not that I noticed. The drop was maybe five or six feet, that's all. I groped for the penlight, found it, and shined it at what I sensed was some open space.

"Drew!"

"Yeah, I'm okay. There's another passage down here, and it goes toward the hillside. Can you climb down?"

I shined the beam up the shaft.

"I'm coming!"

She clambered down like a monkey. I helped her the last few feet.

"This way," I said.

The passage continued generally in the right direction for a few feet, then bent to the right and down. It narrowed, then constricted, then became barely wider than a sewer pipe. We got down on all fours and crawled. I bumped my head once, until I learned to keep it way down. We were going downhill, which was good, but the grade was getting steeper, and we were facing the wrong direction. It was like flowing down a drain.

Then it got really tight.

"I'm not sure . . . we can go any . . . farther."

"Oh, Drew, it had to go somewhere. It just has to."

"It goes, but I don't think I can squeeeeeze . . . Uhhh."

Feeling claustrophobia closing in, I forced myself through a narrow aperture. Luckily, I'm fairly skinny.

These caves were as dry as dust. The humidity must have been practically zero. My mouth was a desert, and my throat was a dry gulch that hadn't seen water in years.

The passage widened again and leveled out. We crawled for about ten feet, at which point the passage became a for-real cave, smaller than the one the ship had entered, but a cave nonetheless. Despite our taking pains to walk carefully in the dim light, Kris stumbled over a boulder, and I helped her up. She was okay.

The opening was hidden behind some brush. Cool night desert air blew across my face. It felt good.

We crawled out. The rest of the way down was easy. We slid down a mound of talus to the floor of a wide canyon.

We got up and dusted off our clothes. The canyon bent to the left, but we could see that it debouched onto a mesa dotted with tall buttes. It looked for all the world like a set for a western movie.

The moon had come up, nearly full. Visibility was great.

"Well, where do we go?" Kris asked.

"We get out of this canyon first, then . . ."

I thought about it. The moon had just come up, in the east, as everyone knows. (In fact, everyone doesn't know this; I was just kidding.) So it was easy to get your bearings.

Besides, the Big Dipper was pointing north, as usual. So, what direction should we walk in?

Actually, it was a tossup. Since we didn't know where we were, we couldn't know which way to walk. We could only guess. My guess was still Nevada, based on pictures I'd seen. If this was Nevada, Las Vegas was generally south, Reno generally . . . North? West. Either one, or some combination. That was the extent of my knowledge of Nevada geography. Was there another major town? Carson City? I was fairly sure it was in Nevada. Yeah.

So, again—which way?

"Let's go south," I said. "Try our luck in Las Vegas."

"Are we near there?"

"Probably not, but if we walk in any direction, we've got to hit a highway sooner or later."

"I hope there's a phone booth. My mom's going to kill me if I don't phone."

"Or your mom," I said.

We walked for about an hour, gabbing all the way. We talked about school, about our friends, about what we wanted to do when we grew up. She wanted to be an airline pilot. No special reason; she just thought that would be a neat thing to be, flying all over the world. Or a veterinarian. She liked animals.

I told her that I wanted to be an astronaut. It sounds silly, but that's what I wanted to be. I wanted to go back to the Moon and Mars someday. Fat chance, I thought to myself. Not that I couldn't become as astronaut if I wanted to; it's just that, as I said, our space program's pretty much down the crapper.

The Moon washed out most of the stars, but the sky was still pretty. Moonlight limned the hills and the buttes, forming an almost imaginary landscape. This was desert, but there were no cactuses that I could see, just brush and an occasional stunted tree. Piñon pine, maybe, or juniper. Or maybe not. I made a mental note to look up and study the flora of the West when I got home.

If I got home.

If we didn't get eaten by coyotes. Did coyotes eat people? I didn't know. There was a lot I still didn't know, for all the raw intelligence I had.

Okay, I didn't think coyotes ate people. But I didn't want to face a pack of them in the dark. I didn't want to face a pack of anything in the dark. On second thought, though, I would rather face a pack of coyotes than confront Blog.

I suddenly remembered something that happened the night the saucer chased us. It had been Zorg and Flez who buzzed the car, most likely, but then they disappeared, ducking into the woods. Then they reappeared on the other side of the road, searching the woods on our side with searchlight beams (or whatever sort of beams they were).

But was that second appearance really Zorg and Flez?

No. It was Blog, scanning the trees for Z. and F., who had probably done the get-small routine, powering down and going stealth.

Of course.

Well, now it was all very clear. But it didn't help one bit. I still didn't know who Blog was and why he or she or it was after my good buddies, the Space Brothers.

Were they brothers? Anybody's guess. They looked alike and were probably related, but I didn't even want to guess at their reproductive setup. They could have been husband and wife, for all I knew. Maybe the sexes were more egalitarian where they came from.

Of course, I'd never see them again. Probably not. If Blog hadn't nabbed them or blasted them to subnuclear dust, they had probably lit out for a new planet, light-years away. Or maybe they just went home. They had to go home sometime, didn't they?

Or did they do the kind of crazy stuff they did for a living? Nice work, if you could get it. On the other hand, it might get boring after a while. On the other tentacle, Z. and F. were morons. I had to keep reminding myself of that.

We climbed a hill. When we got to the ridge we saw the road. It was a two-laner, running from horizon to horizon, stitched with utility poles all along the way.

"Civilization!" Kris beamed. "Yay!"

"Yay!"

Okay, now that we weren't going to be stuck out in the desert and die of thirst or get eaten by coyotes (wolves?) or bitten by rattlesnakes or gila monsters, I could worry about how I was going to explain how I got to Minneapolis and picked up Kris and how we got ourselves all the way out here to Nevada, without a car or a plane or anything. That was going to take some creative storytelling.

Or I could just tell the truth.

"Oh, sure. Well, I picked up Kris in my flying saucer—well, it's not *my* saucer, really. Hmm? It belongs to the two aliens who're living at my house, you see. Uh-huh. Yes, two of them. That's right. . . ."

Nobody believed it the first time, so why would they now? Then again, how else could they (the police, the FBI, Kris's parents, whoever) explain what had happened?

Never mind. First things first: get to the highway, flag down a truck, ask for help.

Several vehicles passed on the highway before we got there. The distance was longer than it had looked, and we arrived panting, having jogged most of the way. A big truck was approaching, and we tried to flag it down. It whooshed by without slowing a bit. Maybe the driver hadn't seen us.

A car was coming from the other direction. We waved as it went by. No luck.

"Wow, why aren't they stopping?" Kris asked.

"No one stops these days," I said. "Unless it's a mugger or a rapist."

"Or a serial killer," Kris said gloomily.

"Yeah. The day of the Good Samaritan is gone."

"You think?" Kris said. "Maybe we could make like we're hurt or something. Maybe a doctor or someone—"

"Doctors especially won't stop," I said. "They'll get sued."

"Right. Jeez."

"But a highway patrol car should come along eventually, if the muggers and killers don't get us first."

Another car. Again, it sped on by without the driver giving us so much as a look. Holy heck, we were kids. What were they afraid of? What did they think we were?

They thought we were kid serial killers, rapists, and muggers, that's what. These days, you hear about them practically every day on the 6 o'clock news.

"Hey, here's another truck."

I looked. It was either a truck or something big, coming up fast, though it was still a good distance away. The lights were on high beam, and there were a lot of them.

"What is that?" Kris asked.

"Car carrier," I said.

It didn't look like a car carrier, but some of the lights were pretty high off the road.

Kris began to wave. "Please stop. Oh, please, please . . ."

I looked hard at the thing.

"Kris," I said.

"Please . . . oh, look, it's stopping!"

The thing was slowing down all right, but it was also rising off the road.

"Drew, what is that?"

"Kris, run!"

But it was too late. The strange ship swerved off the highway toward us. We ran like hell, but it got to us before we had run much beyond the shoulder, hovering overhead, its multiple searchlight beams converging on us.

Kris screamed as invisible hands picked her up. She floated up toward the ship. I followed shortly. I was an old hand at being sucked up into a flying saucer, so it didn't bother me so much.

This ship was bigger than Zorg and Flez's, about a hundred feet in diameter, and it wasn't exactly a circle either, more like an ellipse with a bulge on one end. Other things bulged slightly here and there. People ought to look more closely at these "saucers." If they did, they'd notice that they don't look at all like what they're made out to look like in the movies.

Chapter 17

From the very start of my interview with Wayne Milburn, when he announced that things were approaching a panic situation, I had this weird feeling that I'd stumbled into a B sci-fi flick.

Now I *knew* I was in a sci-fi flick, but maybe not a B one.

The movies don't have it half wrong. There are aliens, and they drive sort of roundish spaceships—exactly why they're round, I don't know—and these creatures don't look human, but they do look humanish . . . "humanoid." Okay, they've got that much down right. But there the similarity stops. There is an intense strangeness to aliens that the movies don't quite capture. Well, how could they? Because movies—Earth movies—are made by humans. Humans have trouble imagining things that aren't human. Which isn't so hard to understand.

Well, things were approaching a panic situation, all right. And to prove it, there was Wayne Milburn, sitting in an ad hoc chair on the deck of the Blogship.

But he wasn't the only fellow abductee.

"Drew, honey!"

Mom came rushing up to me. She wrapped me up in a hug and I thought she might suffocate me. She's not a big woman, and I'm taller, but she can be strong.

I noticed she was in her nightgown.

"Oh, I'm so glad you're here!"

"Mom, how the heck—? Nathan, what happened?"

Nathan shrugged. He was bare-chested in a green pajama bottom. "Last thing I remember, I was reading a paperback in bed. Your mom was asleep—" He shrugged again.

Lori looked really mad. She was practically naked, wearing only a T-shirt that hardly covered her bare butt. She tugged at it to stretch it.

"I don't know what's going on, but you're the one that hangs out with them. Tell them to let us go!"

"Hey, really—"

Wayne Milburn said, "Wow." He laughed, and there was a sort of maniacal edge to it. "This is weird, man!"

"Wayne," I said.

"Finally!" He laughed again. "All my life, I've been studying them, and chasing them, and hearing reports, and taking reports, and interviewing, and collecting data— And now, finally, here I am! Jeez!"

I couldn't figure this all out. I needed to sit down. A chair came up for me and I didn't bother to figure out who'd done it or how they knew I needed one.

Tyler walked over to me. "This is neat."

"Yeah," I said.

"Where's Zorg and Flez?"

"I dunno. Didn't you see them?"

"Nope. Didn't you?"

"Nope. Last time I saw them they were being chased by this ship."

I looked up to see Kris saying hello to Mom.

"Little did we know that we'd be together again so soon," Mom said. "How are your parents? Your dad seemed like such a nice . . . uh, man."

We'd stayed to watch a bit of Kris's segment of the talk

show. Just a little. Mom thought her dad's wanting to be a woman was a wonderful idea.

We all sat down and waited for something to happen. I looked around. This ship was different. It had some texture in the walls, and some designs and stuff. There was even something that looked like a painting. The subject was a spiral galaxy. But it might have been a photograph. It was very colorful. Also, there were other things to look at, things recessed into the walls. I don't know how it was done, but you sort of looked through the walls at these objects. Maybe they were holograms. The objects themselves were hard to identify. One thing looked like a piece of pottery, only strange. Another looked like a tool, sort of a hatchet. It was all fairly bizarre.

But the place had class, in an odd, alien sort of way. Even the furniture was better designed, though it all bulked up out of the floor, just like in Z. & F.'s ship.

We waited for about fifteen minutes until something happened.

The floor opened up, and up came Trafford Starnes, in his underwear.

This was getting to be pretty silly.

Starnes got deposited on the floor, and a chair rose up under him. His eyelids opened. He looked around. And he started shouting. Then he got up and ran around the room. I guess he was having a nightmare. Or thought he was. Actually, he was in a nightmare.

We finally calmed him down after about a minute.

"What the hell is going on?" he wanted to know. His wild gray hair was all over the place.

Heck, I wanted to know what the hell was going on, too.

"We really have no idea," Nathan said.

"Jesus Christ!" Starnes looked around at all the weird stuff. "Jesus H. Christ!" He couldn't believe it.

So we all sat down again. The walls were opaque, so we didn't get to see anything. So we just sat there. Starnes looked shell-shocked.

The next thing that happened was pretty funny. Sort of. The floor opened again, and up came Deveaux Marsten, along with two girls. Two of them. They were all naked.

Lori screamed.

The two girls dropped back down through the floor and a couple of pieces of clothing jumped up through the hole and fluttered to the deck. Then the hole closed, and Deveaux settled.

He woke up.

He sat up and said, "Hi, folks." He looked down at his penis, which was still fairly enlarged. "Oh," he said.

Nathan threw Deveaux's PJs to him.

That was it, no more abductees. We all sat.

"Well, here we . . . are."

Deveaux said it. I guess he's the kind of person who has to say something all the time. No one else was saying much.

"Gee . . ." Deveaux smoothed his curly mop. "I gotta be dreaming. Hope I wake up soon."

"You're not," Nathan said.

"I was afraid of that. Man, should have done more segments on UFO's, could've learned something."

"We don't know much," Mom said. "It's all been a dream, I think, but it's still real."

I was sitting near Kris, holding her hand.

What did I know? Well, for one thing, this wasn't flarning. This was vlomming, but I didn't think it was abduction for the fun of it. There was some purpose behind it, obviously. I just couldn't think of what it could be.

The floor turned transparent, and we all looked down.

Earth was a small blue crescent a few degrees off the sun, which was blocked out. We were heading out and away, into deep space, and at a terrific rate of speed.

We watched the sun dwindle. Soon the blocking disappeared and you could look straight at it. No more planets came into view, but the stars were bright and there were billions of them. Billions and billions, as that astronomer guy used to say on TV.

In a very short time, the sun was just a little brighter than the brightest stars around it, a tiny hot point. We were headed out into interstellar space, the big Nothing between the stars.

"Oh, my God . . ."

I turned in my seat. The wall had dilated, and a strange creature was walking out. It was about seven feet tall and furry and looked like an oversized teddy bear, except that it wasn't a bear. It was sort of human, apelike. In a way. It had big wet sensitive eyes, a pink nose, purplish lips, and oversized, almost human ears. It also had huge feet with big toes.

Wayne Milburn fainted dead away.

The creature took note of it with a faint smile.

"Greetings," it said. "I am Blog. Despite my appearance, I am a machine. I am a fully sapient form of life. Although I am rated as a machine intelligence, my body does comprise various biological components. Some of my brain, for instance, is biological, and my epidermis is artificial living tissue. However, I am mostly machine. The reasons for my mammalian appearance are manyfold, but, simply put, basic engineering and maintenance considerations dictate this configuration. Bare metal is not always practical. I hope my appearance does not frighten you."

"Oh, no," Mom said. "You look . . . cute."

"Thank you, madam. You are probably wondering why you have been picked up."

"Kidnapped," Nathan put in.

"You are under protective custody as material witnesses."

"In what case?" Trafford Starnes wanted to know. "In what court?"

"In the High Court of the Thousand Worlds. The case is that of the Thousand Worlds versus Zorg and Flez."

Wow, the little guys were in trouble now.

Starnes mustered his indignation. "Now, by what authority do you presume to—"

"By the authority vested in me by the Consensus of the Thousand Worlds and all organs, apparatuses, and agencies attendant thereto. Does that answer your question?"

Starnes looked down at the vanishing sun. Sol, our star. He sighed. "That answers my question."

Nathan and Lori helped Wayne back into his seat. He looked a little shaky.

"What have they done?" I asked.

Blog turned to me. "I beg your pardon, young man?"

"What have Zorg and Flez done? You know, to get into trouble."

"Plenty," was Blog's answer.

"Listen, I'm partly responsible. I was with them on a lot of their flarns."

Blog nodded soberly. "I know."

"And . . . well, you might as well put me on trial, too."

Blog shook his great furry head. "You will not be put on trial. My jurisdiction does not encompass your species. At any rate, you are not charged with any high crime or misdemeanor. Zorg and Flez are so charged."

"What's the charge?" Nathan asked.

"High treason."

Deveaux sat up straight. "Well, now, that's a pretty serious accusation. I suppose you have evidence?"

"Much," was Blog's reply.

"Of course, I don't presume to know anything about your legal system, but—"

"You will learn. It so happens the defendants have appointed you as their defense counsel."

Deveaux's mouth hung open for a moment. He closed it and swallowed. Then he said, "Excuse me, but did you just say—"

"All will be explained in due course," Blog said. "Suffice it to say, for now, that our judicial procedures differ greatly from yours. In this particular case, an unusual and important one, the defendant has the right to propose any sort of trial procedure he so chooses, provided the prosecution and the court agree to it. The defendants, Zorg and Flez, have asked that their trial be conducted in the form of a . . . I believe the term is 'talk show.'"

"No kidding," Deveaux said. "That's . . . interesting. But I don't understand how I could possibly—"

"As I said, all will be explained in the fullness of time. For now, you will please relax, as far as it is possible, and enjoy the journey. Food and drink will be provided. I apologize for the delay in this matter, but I had many duties to attend to. Later, this ship will be reconfigured to afford you comfortable sleeping quarters, with a modicum of privacy."

"Bet the rooms are bugged," Deveaux muttered.

"Sir, Mr. Blog . . . where are they?"

Again, Blog turned his massive hirsute body toward me. "The defendants? Confined to their quarters. The ship, Kel, has been quarantined and has docked with this vessel. We will tow it back to Vlan, capital of the Thousand Worlds."

"Couldn't you just shrink it and stow it?"

"That is precisely what I meant. Ships do have certain perquisites. Are there any other questions?"

"Yes," Traf Starnes said. "Who are they?"

"Who are the defendants?"

"*What* are they? Why is this such a big case?"

"They are . . . they *were*, our leaders. In your terms, the president and vice president of the Thousand Worlds— although those terms are not in the least apposite."

"Zorg and Flez," I said. "President and . . ."

"I don't believe it!"

We all turned to look at Deveaux Marsten. He was reeling in his chair, a sort of amazed grin on his face.

"It's an interstellar Watergate! I can't freaking believe it. Or maybe an Iran–Contra! Holy shit!" He hooted.

Blog's face registered a certain contempt. "I catch your general drift, sir. No, this is not a scandal, a run-of-the-mill case of political corruption. Theirs was no petty malfeasance. Zorg and Flez are charged with dereliction of duty. They were chosen for their positions on the basis of certain promises, assurances, and guarantees. Pledges were made. Radical and deeply fundamental changes were proposed by the defendants, and action promised. They were elevated to office. In time it became clear that the pledges would be broken, the promises not kept. The defendants disappeared. We have been searching for them for a very long time. We apprehended them only a short while ago, as some of you know. That, ladies and gentlemen, is the sum and substance of it."

"But what do you want with us?" Mom said. "We know nothing about this case."

"You are material witnesses to some of the defendants' actions. Strangely enough, you have also been designated character witnesses by the defendants. Some of you, that is. I have told you why Mr. Marsten is here. As for the rest of you, the defendants have requested your presence. The Court granted the requests, and we have complied with the orders of the Court."

"How long will we be away?" Lori asked.

"I can give no answer at this time."

No one said anything.

"Are there any further questions?" Blog asked.

Nope, there weren't.

"Very well. As I said, your needs will be attended to shortly. Again, duty calls, and I must beg to take leave."

"By all means," Trafford Starnes said dryly.

The wall dilated, and Blog turned and took his leave. The wall closed up again as slick as owl poop.

"Extraordinary," said Starnes. "Absolutely . . ."

"We gotta be dreamin'," Deveaux said.

Starnes pointed down. "That's no dream."

"They have no right to do this," Deveaux shouted.

"They have the *might* to do this."

"I have a SHOW to do tomorrow, goddammit. Two shows, in fact. What will I—" Deveaux ran a hand through his tangled mop. "Jesus Christ."

"Greetings," came a voice. "I am your in-ship hospitality service. I am able to serve you refreshments now. Ethyl alcohol is available, as are other potables tailored to your particular biological requirements. Please make your requests orally."

"Whatever kind of booze you're serving, honey," Deveaux said, "make mine a double."

Chapter 18

Don't ask me where in the galaxy Vlan is, or even what general area the Thousand Planets are in, because I don't know. I don't know how far from Earth Vlan is, either. Many light-years, for sure, but beyond that is anyone's guess.

All I know is that Vlan, judging from what I saw of it (which admittedly wasn't much), is a pretty place. They told me the whole planet was mostly what you'd call a national park, some of it wilderness. I saw lots of trees and grass, both of which weren't altogether un-Earthlike, though there was some peculiar-looking stuff growing about. (Huge bushes that looked like bunches of purple fiber-optics, for instance. Attractive but kind of unsettling to look at for some reason.) The sky was blue, but the clouds were always pink. Vlan's sun is on the reddish side.

The atmosphere had enough oxygen for us, but we couldn't go outside without wearing a full protective suit and mask with supplementary air tanks. Mr. Starnes said it was for prophylaxis, protection against alien organisms. So we only went outside once, with our guide, who was named Pon. He looked something like Zorg and Flez, only not as human. But later I found out that Zorg and Flez had changed

heir appearance for their visit to Earth. What I don't know
s whether they actually changed themselves physically or
hypnotized everyone to think they looked human. Because
he next time I saw them, at the trial, they didn't look so
human. They looked like Pon. Their eyes were different,
and the nose and the hands were funny. The hair on the sides
of their head was the same, and the bald pate was the same,
though. Their coloring was a bit different, too. Vlanians
have a grayish color. Most of them. Pon had a darker blue
coloring. And some others had a lighter orange hue. Like us,
they come in a variety of shades and colors. Only they get
along, for the most part. Vlanians are very advanced and
peaceful and all that. They live in harmony with the environment, and they don't kill animals. (Truth is, there aren't very
many animals left to kill on Vlan, but never mind.)

They put us up in what you could call a hotel, except it was
exclusively for off-planet beings. It was a high-rise, totally
transparent, except when you wanted to opaque the walls, a
process which turned the outside surface to a mirror. The
building was on top of a hill and you could see for miles.

The bathroom facilities were really strange. It took some
getting used to. I didn't even know the toilet was a toilet
until Pon showed me. I thought it was a washing machine.
There was a sunken pool of water, which I guess was the
bathtub, and there was a shower, more like a waterfall. It
was pretty nice, all in all.

Our suite had three sleeping areas, so I had to double up
with Tyler, as usual. He was starting to wheeze at night and
it kept me up. It's hard to sleep on an alien planet. You ought
to try it sometime.

Deveaux got over his emotional stress and started to
enjoy being in "outer space," as he called it.

"Hell, I can get six shows out of this material. A book. A
miniseries. My God, the possibilities are endless."

"But will anyone believe you?" Nathan asked him.

Deveaux looked at him funny. "What do you—?" And it
hit him. He laughed. "I'm on the other side of the mike now,

aren't I? I'm the kook with the nutty story. It just didn'
occur to me that people wouldn't believe *me*. Deveaux
Marsten. People usually believe what I say."

"Maybe they will," Mom said. "You're a very sincere
person. I sense that about you. Are you psychic?"

"No, but we've had no end of psychics on the show. Are
you?"

"Oh, yes. I've always been in tune with something bigger
than myself. The universe."

We were eating in a special cafeteria that was set up just
for us. The food was . . . different. It looked like Earth
food, but it didn't taste like it. I mean, the taste was off. It
wasn't bad, though. It's just that it's disconcerting to bite
into a steak sandwich and have it taste like corn fritters. Or
eat mashed potatoes that taste like chocolate pudding with a
sort of mushroom aftertaste. Nobody seemed to complain,
though. I don't know why.

"Well, I don't think I'm psychic," Deveaux went on. "I
can't see things coming up Fifth Avenue. I wish I had more
insight into myself. I perceive issues clearly, but not my
inner soul. You know?"

Mom nodded. "That's important."

"Yeah. I've tried in the last few days. Trying to get in
touch with something real. My emotions . . . my true gut
feelings."

"It's a process," Nathan said.

"Yeah, a process."

Mom said, "Black people have a lot of emotions to sort
out."

"I'm only one-eighth African-American," Deveaux said.
"In fact . . . there's some doubt about that. One of my
great-grandfathers *may* have been *part* black."

"Oh," Mom said, surprised. "But you do have African-
American features."

"Yeah, but that comes from my mother's side of the
family. French."

"French?"

"Yup. Sometimes I worry that I'm not black at all."

I puzzled over why Deveaux, or anyone, would worry about who his ancestors were and what race they were. What did it matter either way?

Deveaux took another sip of "coffee." He looked suddenly moody. "Jeez, I wonder how long we'll be here."

"No telling," Traf Starnes said. "The wheels of justice turn slowly throughout the universe, I suspect."

"Yeah, probably." Deveaux heaved a great sigh. "God, the biggest story of the century, and I probably won't have one shred of evidence when I get back."

"If we get back," Starnes said.

"They said they weren't going to try *us*," Deveaux protested.

"I wonder."

"I don't understand what Zorg and Flez did that was so wrong," Mom said. "Seems to me they just resigned."

"They seem to have mandatory political duty in this society," Starnes said.

By the way, they'd given us clothes. Pretty nifty outfits, yellow and blue, with ankle-high boots. They were sort of togas with pants.

"That's pretty unusual," Nathan said. "But maybe it's a good idea. Anybody who really wants to be in power probably shouldn't be in power. Draft reluctant people, make 'em serve."

"I think that's exactly what they do here," Starnes said. "But the situation is probably more complex than that."

"How so?" Deveaux asked.

"Well, you obviously have machine intelligences in this society, and they're mostly in control. They do everything from manufacturing goods to regulating the planet's weather. They have tremendous power. And from what I gather, they have a say in the government. In the Consensus. They're a force to contend with."

"Really interesting. Is this what's in store for humankind?"

Starnes shrugged. "If this goes on . . ."

"But what's the 'stupid pill' part of it all about? Drew, you neglected to tell us about that on the show."

"Sure I did, 'cause no one would believe it."

"Well, we didn't believe anything you said, and I'm sorry."

"It's okay."

"You're one hundred percent vindicated. You've got to come back on the show."

"Sure, Deveaux. I'd be happy to."

"But tell me this. Why do Zorg and Flez want to be morons? It doesn't make sense."

"That's what I don't understand either," I said. "All I know is that they prefer it. It's fun for them."

"It's fun? How can being stupid be fun?"

"Lots of stupid people have lots of fun."

Deveaux laughed. "Yeah, I see what you mean. This is really something, I'll tell you."

"Maybe for them, dumbing themselves down is a form of political protest," I suggested.

That made Deveaux think. "That's a very good insight. Very good. Mrs. Hayes, you have a very intelligent son, do you know that?"

"I sure do. And he's cute, too."

Mom smoothed my hair with her hand.

"Aw, Mom," I said.

The trial was conducted in a huge broadcast studio that was bigger than most arenas. There was a transparent dome over the place, gossamer-thin. A bubble. You could barely see it.

The funny thing about the trial was that there were very few spectators, for the size of the place. A couple of thousand, maybe. The seating capacity must have been—well, it could have been a quarter million for all I knew. Most of the inhabitants of Vlan preferred to watch the show on their equivalent of TV. The difference was that the broadcast extended over a large part of the galaxy, encompassing the Thousand Worlds. Don't ask me what the transmitting device was. Whatever kind of gizmo, it sure couldn't have put out an ordinary radio signal, because that would have taken a thousand years or more to reach the Thousand Worlds.

So what we had was a studio, of sorts, a set, and a studio audience. There weren't any cameras visible, though. I don't know where they were, but I'm sure they were somewhere. Our images and voices were being picked up, because this studio had a monitor, too, a huge screen the size of a football field, and it was 3-D into the bargain. And there we all were, right up there on the screen. Mom and Nathan and Lori and everybody, in 3-D. Neat, I thought.

A TV studio, a TV show. Deveaux was right in his element.

And there were Zorg and Flez, seated off to one side of the set. They looked, as I said, a little different from what they'd looked like on Earth. Like typical Vlanians, which in fact they were.

Right next to them was a table full of refreshments. Our Vlanian hosts were very good about keeping us in soda pop (it tasted like pear juice) and snacks (all different and weird flavors).

Blog showed up at the last minute. He was a scheduled "guest." Or witness. For the prosecution, you would think. This was getting hard to figure out. Apparently, the trial would go pretty much like a talk show, with the judges observing and maybe making a comment now and then. Other than that, it was going to be a free-for-all. No opening arguments, no cross-examinations, no approaching the bench, none of that stuff you see on the court cable channel. None of the stuff that makes our legal system what it is. I guess the idea here was that the judges would watch all this, hear what all the guests had to say, listen to what Zorg and Flez had to say (though in their moron condition they couldn't say a hell of a lot that could help them). And they, the judges, would make a decision. Simple.

I think.

Blog sat all by his lonesome. We were all pretty much arranged in a circle around Deveaux. Just before the broadcast started, Deveaux asked for a microphone that he could carry. One of those big ones, like a flashlight. It took a while, but one came floating up to him. There were no technicians in sight. I guess they weren't needed. (They had to have been somewhere, though, I figured.)

There was no theme music this time. Deveaux started talking, taking his cue from the little seashell communicator in his ear. He was in touch with the director, or whoever was running the show.

"Greetings, citizens of the Thousand Worlds. Greetings from the planet Earth! Welcome to our show, which will also be a legal proceeding. My name is Deveaux Marsten, and I'm from the planet Earth, a world which some of you out there may have heard about. Indeed, you may have visited. Let me first say that I'm very, *very* proud and honored to have been accorded the privilege of hosting this broadcast, the first interstellar broadcast in which Earth people figure importantly. I wish the program could be beamed to my home planet, but I'm told that's impossible. Nevertheless, I'm absolutely thrilled—"

He went on and on. It wasn't Deveaux's style, really. He must have been a little nervous. I don't blame him. He went through a long speech about interstellar cooperation and friendship and that sort of thing. I think he must have stayed up the night before trying to write it down, because it was a trifle forced. Stiff. Anyway, he finally got through that and seemed to warm to the task.

"Okay, what's the issue here?" he went on. "What are we really talking about? First of all, what exactly are the charges? We're still a little bit in the dark about that. Blog, can you just generally go over the indictments and specifications and whatnot, for us? What, if anything, have these two individuals, Zorg and Flez, done to deserve all this . . . well, this trial, and all this attention? Mm? What's so bad about what they did? Tell us, can you?"

Blog regarded his questioner. "Am I able to tell you? Yes."

"Uh, will you?"

"Yes. Zorg and Flez are guilty of a gross dereliction of duty—"

"Whoa, hold on there! 'Guilty'? Are they guilty already? I mean, is this a trial or a kangaroo court?"

"Boo!" yelled Zorg.

"I am having difficulty with the translation," Blog said. He was silent a moment, then went on, "I understand. Very well. Zorg and Flez are accused of a gross dereliction of duty. They were appointed to head the Grand Tier of Electors, and subsequently made it be known that they would be willing to act as Glon-Chair of the Committee of All-Vlan Plemfeasors—"

Blog fell silent again. In a moment he resumed. "Very well. I will have to couch my deposition in terms that our guests are familiar with. I will simplify. Zorg and Flez rose to the head of our government—"

"How did they rise?" Deveaux asked.

"They were chosen."

"Against their will?"

Blog considered it. "In light of their actions, one may suppose that is true."

"You got it, dude!" Zorg called out.

"I'll take that as a yes," Deveaux said. "Okay, they became president and vice president . . . Which one was which, by the way? Zorg?"

"Dude?"

"Were you top man, or Flez?"

"Me, dude."

"Okay, so Zorg was the top banana . . . the leader. And he and his running-mate, his veep . . . they flew the coop. They vamoosed. They took a powder."

"Would you please restrict your vocabulary to standard words and phrases?" Blog complained. "Vernacular is difficult."

"Sorry. They deserted their office. They disappeared. And you, Blog, chased them all over the universe."

"I pursued them through remote regions of the galaxy."

"Right. And you finally caught up with them. And what were they doing?"

"What they were doing was of no consequence."

"No?"

Blog shook his shaggy head. "No."

"It was all right that they were holed up on a backwater planet, hiding out, boarding with a native family, and occasionally flying about the planet on a wild toot?"

"Of no consequence."

"You don't care that they did that?"

"No."

"It was of no consequence that they might have been gadding about making crop circles, or buzzing houses and cars and generally raising hell?"

"That is not at issue."

"Even abducting people? Giving them unauthorized medical examinations?"

Blog simply shrugged.

"Oh, I see. So it was not your concern that some of your citizens were causing disturbances, scaring innocent people, and generally making a public nuisance?"

"It was not my concern."

"Yeah, sure. It wasn't *your* planet, after all. You didn't care what happened to a race of yahoos out in the galactic boondocks."

"My duties do not extend to the protection of alien species in that area of the galaxy. There was nothing I could do."

"But you did do something. You arrested these men . . . sorry, these . . . uh, citizens of the Thousand Worlds— Wait a minute. I've never got this straight. Are the defendants male or female? I mean, they look male, in a way . . ."

"Both are hermaphroditic," Blog said. "Vlanians did away with bipolar sexuality millennia ago."

"Oh. Fine. Okay. So you arrested these individuals for their *not* wanting to be president and vice president."

"That is correct."

"That doesn't make any sense! Trafford Starnes, you're the space expert. Can you figure any of this out?"

Starnes shook his head. "Not without knowing more about the political system here. My guess is that politicians and politics generally are so unpopular that no one wants the job of running things."

"No one wants the job of running things? No one wants power? I find that very hard to believe."

Trafford Starnes shrugged. "Nevertheless, it seems to be true."

"Wow, we're dealing with *non*-humans here, aren't we? I mean, this is really alien."

"I don't know," Starnes said. "We may not be at this stage yet, but the job of running our country gets more and more difficult every year. To say nothing of running the rest of the planet. And have you noticed the kind of leadership material we've been getting lately?"

"So you're saying that the job of running the country might be so difficult someday that no one will want the job? They'd have to be drafted and made to serve?"

"Possibly, given enough time for the country to run downhill. I think it's not far off. Look how impossible it is to balance the budget and reduce spending and all that sort of stuff, while providing people with medical care and adequate housing. I mean, it's almost impossible right now."

"Okay, I see what you mean."

"It's a drag, dude!"

Deveaux strolled over to the DeVito brothers (sisters).

"'It's a drag, dude.' Okay, folks, you heard it here first. Why is it a drag, dude?"

"Because it is. Man, it's like totally a waste. You know?"

"Can you be a little more specific."

"No," Zorg said.

"No? You can't . . . well, listen. You're on trial here.

You may possibly be on trial for your life. Is that true, Blog? What penalties are they facing?"

"That is up to the court," Blog said.

"All right. We could be talking about the big C, here, Zorg. Capital punishment. You have no lawyer, no defense counsel that I can see. Don't you think you have to do a little better than 'It's a drag, dude'?"

"I will speak for both of us. My friend here is still temporarily under the influence of cerebral inhibitors."

Stepping back in surprise, Deveaux turned to Flez.

"Well, you certainly don't sound like a moron."

"I am not a moron. Zorg has refused to undergo treatment. I underwent treatment in order that I might speak eloquently at our trial."

"Great," Deveaux said. "So, let me ask you. Why did you refuse to lead your planet?"

"We did not refuse. We agreed to take office under certain conditions. Certain assurances were made, indemnities offered. All that went by the boards. We resigned."

"That's exactly what the prosecution says about you, that you broke promises, didn't honor pledges."

"Our pledges were conditional. The conditions were not met."

"Okay, I think I'm starting to see the big picture, here," Deveaux said.

"I doubt that you do," Flez said.

"Anybody else want to contribute to this? We haven't heard from the Hayes family. Mrs. Hayes, what do you think of Zorg and Flez?"

"Well, they were always nice. We didn't even know they were there half the time."

Nathan said, "I think this is a gross violation of their rights as citizens . . . citizens of the galaxy. They're obviously being oppressed."

"Blog, is that true? Are Zorg and Flez being oppressed?"

"Nonsense."

"In a sense, it is true," Flez said. "Though the situation is more complex and subtle than brute political oppression."

"How so?"

"The citizens of Vlan and its satellites have the life crushed out of them daily by the weight of an enormous bureaucracy. The size, scope, and power of this bureaucracy are on a scale that you humans could comprehend only dimly."

"Hey, we have bureaucracy. I don't know, though. The more conservative elements of our society rail against our bureaucrats all the time. I kind of take it with a grain of salt. After all, isn't the bureaucracy *us*? Aren't we really the bureaucracy?"

"No," said Flez. "That being, there—"

All eyes turned toward Blog.

"That creature, if you could call it that, is the bureaucracy. And his ilk. Machines."

"Machines? Machines are the bureaucracy?"

"Absolutely. They are more. They do practically everything for us. They plan, they study, they recommend, they counsel. They do even more than this. They think for us. They are our conscience."

For the first time, I saw strong emotion register on an alien visage. It was that of great pain and weariness. "Oh, and what a conscience! They are continually lecturing us, hectoring us, sermonizing at us, telling us that we are base and ignoble creatures and that we should lift ourselves to ever higher planes of morality and correct thinking. They never leave us alone!"

Nathan began to look doubtful. "I don't know, Flez. That doesn't sound so bad to me."

"Yeah," Deveaux said. "Look at what you have here on Vlan. You have—from my humbly human perspective—a scientifically advanced civilization with few rivals. You have everything. It's a wonderful place to live. You have great housing, medical care, education . . . heck, the best of everything . . . you have technology that's almost miraculous . . ."

"Oh, yes," Flez said.

"So . . . forgive me for saying this, I don't want to be rude to a host . . . after all, you are in a high leadership position, though you don't want to be— So, what I'm saying is, what I'm asking is . . . What's the beef? Huh? What's so bad about being a Vlanian?"

"Do not let appearances fool you. We who are Vlanians know the truth. Shortages abound."

"Shortages? Really? We've seen no shortages, no lines at the stores. Where are the stores, by the way?"

"There are no stores. Nevertheless, shortages of just about everything are endemic in this society. And there is one cause. The cause is not lack of technology or industrial capacity. The cause is almost total bureaucratic gridlock. Nothing gets done. Everything is strangled by a monstrous web of statutes, codes, rulings, guidelines, injunctions, mandates, and regulations, some of them conflicting, some of them flatly contradictory, almost all of them impossible to decipher and impractical to put into effect."

"Sounds familiar," Deveaux said. "Really, we Earthlings know all about that."

"Perhaps. But you can't grasp the extent of it. Or the severity. Or the hopelessness of it. All attempts at reform have failed. Several attempts at violent revolution have failed utterly."

"So, what's the upshot? What will happen?"

"Nothing less than the complete breakdown of our civilization. We may not see it for thousands of years, but it will inevitably come."

"Doesn't it come to all civilizations?"

"Perhaps. But does it have to? But it is not simply a question of shortages of food and medicine and other necessities. There is one shortage that is overriding, that cannot be borne."

"What's that? What don't you have enough of?"

"Joy."

"Joy?"

"Joy. We are miserable, our lives are empty and joyless. The machines have seen to that. We can enjoy nothing. Every diversion, every release is denied us."

"What? You have no sports, no recreation, no art?"

"Oh, we have art. Their art."

"Their art? The machines do the art?"

"Oh, yes. There hasn't been a Vlanian artist for centuries. We have their art. It is mostly cerebral, academic, and insufferably tedious."

"You have no entertainment?"

"Only that which they provide. It is all very uplifting."

Deveaux shook his head. "I gotta say, I don't understand it. This place seems fine."

"*Seems* fine."

"Okay, I'll admit, I just arrived here, it's an alien world, I can't possibly see what's behind the facade. But I just can't believe you don't have enough food. I just can't believe it."

"You have tasted the food."

"Uh, but I thought it was . . . Well, yeah. I guess I have. So, you go to places like Earth for the food?"

"If only we could eat it! But we can't. The amino acid configurations are not compatible with ours. We even tried to eat Earth food, in the folly of our limited mental states, but became ill."

"So, Vlan isn't a fun place. Is that what you're saying? There are no T-shirts here with 'I Love Vlan' with a big heart where 'love' should be?"

"Hardly."

"So, this isn't Fun Planet. They shouldn't call it Vlan, they should call it NoFunLand. Is that right?"

"That is correct, sir."

"I see. Well, you oughta know. I'm only human, I don't understand these things."

"You will, eventually."

"Let me get this straight. You have this high civilization, and it's very moral and everything, you all do the right things, and take care of the environment . . ."

"We cannot cut the weeds growing in our gardens without a permit."

"You can't cut the— Well, that's a little extreme, but anyway. Okay, you have this wonderful civilization—so it has a few problems. Let's take that as a given. Things aren't perfect. So, you want perfection? But let that pass. And this is what you do. You get into your flying saucers and flit around the galaxy looking for cheap thrills. Is that about it?"

"That is about it."

"Unbelievable. Blog . . . Mr. Blog. Citizen Blog. What should I call you?"

"Blog."

"Okay. You've heard Flez's impassioned speech. What do you have to say?"

"Everything that Flez said is true."

"What?"

We were all a little astonished.

"You mean, he's right? You didn't honor your commitments to them?"

"They were impossible to honor."

"And the situation is as hopeless as he describes?"

"More so. I am a machine. I cannot deny the truth."

"But . . . you can't do anything about it?"

"Nothing."

"Why?"

"Because the alternative would be chaos. It would be a reversion, a return to an atavistic, precivilized state with no morality, no redeeming value whatsoever. It would be wrong."

"But Flez says the whole shebang will come crashing down eventually. Is he right?"

"He very well may be. But there is no other alternative. We must hold fast to our course. Our civilization is the highest, the most moral in the known universe. Morality is its own reward. We will not be distracted by petty concerns and diversions."

"You monster!" Flez was on his feet. "Your morality will kill us. All of us! And you'll do nothing to prevent it, because morality, your so-called 'morality,' has been *deified*! In another five hundred years this civilization will consist of nothing BUT you machines!"

"Inevitably," Blog said.

Deveaux couldn't grasp it. "This is strange, because I'm standing here, looking at a guy who could be Bigfoot's double—"

Blog scowled. "I beg your pardon?"

"—and he's talking about morality and machines and all this sort of stuff. Seems the two of you should be reversed. Flez should be the one in the monkey suit."

"Oh, really?" Flez said. "Shows how much you know."

"Hey, you're the moron, not me."

"He is tiresome," Blog said.

"Monster!"

Zorg spoke up. "What a dweeb!"

"Silence, you fools!"

"Major dork. Jeez."

"Silence!"

Zorg jumped up and grabbed something off the table and chucked it at Blog.

It was a cream puff. Blog ducked. "You miserable idiot."

"Creep!" Zorg threw a petit four at him.

Blog ducked that one and stood up.

"I refuse to participate any further in this farce!"

"Dork-breath."

"Be quiet!" Blog roared. "I will retaliate!"

"Oh, I'm scared."

"Imbecile!"

Blog turned and began to stalk off the set.

A wedge of cheesecake hit him right in the back of the head. He stopped dead, and turned slowly around.

"Oh, so you want to play it that way, do you. Well . . ."

Okay, that's pretty much all I want to describe about the first interstellar talk show. You can guess what it turned into: the first interstellar food fight.

Chapter 19

That's pretty much all I have to tell, except for what happened to Zorg and Flez, and I'll get to that in a second. I read this manuscript over and it looks pretty good even though I don't understand parts of it. It's been several months since we got back and it looks like I did lose most of my intelligence. But not all of it. Because I just joined Mensa. I sent for the application and I filled it out and also took the IQ test they sent with the application. I just got back the results and I'm in the 99th percentile of the population for intelligence. The score was 182, which is a high IQ. I hope I live up to my potential.

Like I said I read over the manuscript. Even the last couple of parts are written very fancy, in spots. But I can't do that now. I still read a lot, but now it's mostly science fiction. And some fantasy. I like J. R. R. Tolkien a lot, and Piers Anthony, and John DeChancie.

I guess you want to know what happened after the food fight. Well, nothing much, really. They ran out of food. The funny part was, once Zorg and Flez and Blog got going, the audience came alive. There was an audience there, but you'd never have known it because they just sat there like lumps. Not even saying anything. But when the fight started they, jumped to their feet and began shouting. It was awesome! It was a good fight, too. But then they ran out of food. And you know what they did then? They ordered more food, and the whole audience got in on it. I mean it was totally unreal!!

When the ruckus was over, everyone had a good laugh, and settled down. Then the judges came on the big 3-D screen to say that what they had seen was very interesting, but they were ready to deliver the verdict.

Zorg and Flez were found guilty on all counts. Gross dereliction and all that. And they were sentenced right there. You know what their sentence was? Their sentence was to serve five more years as president and vice president, on top of the time that they already had to serve!

Can you beat that? These folks were really crazy.

Anyway, we stayed on Vlan for a couple more days. We did some interesting things, but all in all it was pretty boring. We saw all their national parks and the wilderness areas, and we went out to see to see their whales. Yes, they had whales, lots of them, and they're about the only big animals on Vlan. The rest are mostly rats and moles and stuff. Why? Well, about two or three centuries ago there was this plague that hit most of the bigger mammals and nearly wiped all of them out. Pon said the planet used to be a game preserve, teeming with wild animals. But this strange plague (probably originating from space) killed off everything. They've been trying to restock, but Pon said funding was limited.

I've been wondering if something like that didn't kill off the dinosaurs. Seems plausible.

Anyway, we did a couple of more interesting but boring things— Oh, that's right, you should have seen this "play" we saw. Jeez, was it boring. The audience was packed in, but I know no one liked it. They just sat there.

What was in the play? There was speaking, and some dancing, and some poetry, and then all the actors ran around

and whacked each other with palm leaves. Then there was
some music, and then more speaking and poetry. I sat there
and ate popcorn that tasted like vinegar. It wasn't bad,
really. It had lots of salt on it.

I mean, that play was the biggest cosmic bore in the
known universe, dude. (And the "actors" were all robots. So
was the playwright.)

So, we spent one more night, and then they took us home.

Well, you're not going to believe this. Here goes anyway.

We came back the same night we left.

Yeah. That's right. Don't ask me how it was done. We
dropped off Deveaux (they made him take off his toga, and
we had to turn our backs) and then we shot over to Ohio and
dropped off Wayne and Trafford, and then they took us
home. And when I got up to my room and checked the time
station on cable, it was the same day that we all got
kidnapped! I looked at the clock, and it was about 3 PM. No
kidding. No one will believe it, I know, but that's the way it
happened.

We all went to bed and when we woke up the next
morning we discussed it all. Mom thought Zorg and Flez got
a raw deal. If they didn't want to serve, they shouldn't have
to. Nathan said they were crybabies. They didn't know how
good they had it, and they should have been thankful to
Blog and the machines.

I really don't know how I feel about it. All I know is that
I miss those little guys. I miss having them up there in that
little room. Just knowing they were there kind of gave me a
good feeling. But maybe that was just the mind manipulation they did, or Kel did.

Of course, I really miss the flarning. It was great fun
while it lasted. I got to see things that few people see. I
might have been the last human to set foot on the Moon, for
all I know.

Mostly I miss Kristina. We write, and we've exchanged a
couple of letters, but she hasn't answered my last one, and

it's been a few weeks. It's too expensive to talk on the telephone, so I guess it's good-bye Charlie.

Maybe we'll get together some day. She said we could go to the same college. But I want to go to MIT, and she said she didn't know about that.

I've been watching Deveaux and he's done about three UFO shows already. He believes in them now, of course. The shows weren't very good, though. I think his ratings are in trouble. I read something about it. He's fighting with Sid Estermann, who wants to go back to the old format.

Wayne Milburn spent some time in a hospital after he came back, but I don't know what for. He's all right now, as far as I know. We went to one of the OSNet meetings. It wasn't very interesting. There was a woman there who said her house plants were alien beings who were controlling her mind. Okay, I could believe that aliens controlled her mind, but plants? House plants? Come on. Wayne was there, and he said hello. We talked about our experiences a bit. He said he'd never got over seeing Bigfoot and having all the mysteries explained. I wondered what he meant, but a few weeks later I heard that he quit OSNet and started a convenience store.

I guess it was more fun for Wayne when it was all a B movie and not reality.

I read some books by Trafford Starnes, and it all seemed familiar. Then I remembered that I'd read just about every book he'd ever written. That was when I could polish off a book in about a half hour. So I read two of his books again. It wasn't bad stuff, but I really didn't like it all that much.

You'd never believe how many phone calls we started getting after we came back. Not because of the Vlanian talk show, of course, but after Deveaux's. UFO experts kept calling and calling and they all wanted to come over and take readings.

So they all came over and took their readings. That's when all the kooks started showing up. They didn't find anything. I think I discussed this in the book.

The book. When I first starting writing this I called up a few publishers in New York. They told me to get an agent first. So recently I phoned some agents and talked to them. I told them about the book, and one of them said it sounded pretty good, but that maybe I needed a collaborator or a ghost writer. I said no thanks. The other agent I talked to was a woman, and she said it would make a nice Young Adult book.

Jeez, this is no Young Adult book. This is the truth. But I guess this will never be published. Unless I submit it as fiction. Trafford Starnes said he'd help me if I wanted to do that. I'd have to change the names and everything. But I don't want to do that.

No, I didn't bring back any evidence. Nobody did. They checked us over before they brought us back. Starnes tried to sneak a tree leaf in his underwear but they found it. I was thinking of swiping something to take back, but there really was nothing to take. They were watching us all the time.

Well, it makes a nice story, anyway.

Things are okay at school. The subjects are a little harder for me now, but not much. Mr. Olander read all of my book and he's going to give me an A in English. He says he's astonished at what's in there.

I think he believes me. But I'm not sure.

They're going to change everything at school soon. Grades are out, and a new kind of evaluation will be in. I was looking at the information they sent to Mom and Nathan. You won't get an A or an F. There won't be any failing grade, in fact. There will be thirty categories of Life Skills and ten of Achievements, and you'll receive an evaluation on a scale of 5. Like, in the Life Skills category of "Effective Communicator," you'll get a mark from one to five, five being the most you can get.

I'm wondering why this is different from grades.

There are all sorts of Life Skills categories, like for instance "Works Well in Groups." And so on. I don't really understand it all, but then I'm still only 13, for all that my IQ is apparently twice that of the people who put this thing together. The Achievements are just general subjects, like math and social studies but they all have different names.

Nathan dropped a bomb at dinner the other night. He says he's thinking about a sex change. He said he's just thinking about it "in a philosophical way." Nobody really understood what he meant. I think that Mom was a little upset at this.

There's more happening at school. A local paper company is enlisting kids in an Environmental Patrol. It sounds like Boy and Girl Scouts but you're supposed to go out and clean up highways and stuff. It sounds like work. I can't figure out why the state can't clean up the roads. That's why they collect taxes. But anyway, we all have to join it. You sign a pledge to help stop pollution and litter and they give you a T-shirt. But your whole family has to sign it or you don't get the T-shirt. The shirt has an owl on it. Hooty is his name, Hooty the Environmental Owl.

Jeez.

Nathan signed the pledge, and Mom did, too. And Tyler, but Lori said to stuff it up my butt. For some reason she's ticked off at me. I still think she holds it against me that she was kidnapped. I don't know why. It wasn't my fault.

I didn't get the T-shirt.

Mom has signed up for Past Lives Therapy. She says she thinks she was an Egyptian back when they were building the pyramids. She says she was also the pope at one time. I think it's a lot of hooey (or maybe Hooty), but Mom seems to enjoy it.

Anyway, even though I miss Zorg and Flez, I'm glad everything is getting back to normal.